The Edge of Awakening

Also by Alanna J. Faison

The Rayne Whitmore Series

The Unmaking

Killer Rayne

The Edge of Awakening

The Soul Tamer Series

The Edge of Awakening

Alanna J. Faison

Published 2017

ISBN 978-0692795040

Cover Artist Alanna J. Faison

Published through www.Createspace.com

For Gram

Maybe one day I'll see Paris…

Chapter One

Death chased me in the form of a monster. I thought that creatures like that only existed in nightmares. But, I saw it with my own eyes. I felt its rough skin, like jagged rocks, rip into my leg just as I nearly made it to safety as I attempted to hide from the beast. I smelled its rancid scent like road-kill baking too long in the sun, as it dragged me across my parent's floor. I peered empty eye sockets as I screamed and kicked and cried and begged for mercy. Then, it slit my throat and I felt pain and fear unlike anything one could ever describe.

I remember the blood. I remember choking for air that refused to fill my lungs and the horrible gurgle of my life force leaking out through the wound. The pain, I still remember the pain as the thing cut me open. I knew that I was dying and the only thing I could think about was wishing that I could die quicker so that the pain would disappear. It seemed to be an endless ocean of suffering for me. Wave after wave of agony that drowned out any hope of ever being saved.

Then, the world went black as a bottomless pit and there was nothing. I stepped into a void where there was nothing to see. Complete darkness. I imagine that's what hell is actually like. Emptiness, darkness, nothingness forever and ever. At least, for some of the terrible people in the world. For me, the darkness became the light of two suns. Yet, the vast emptiness was still there. Is still here. Suspended in an empty world, I float in and out of consciousness.

I can't recall who I am, what's become of me. I almost forget. That is, until I remember. I remember it all over again. Something evil chased me. A horrible monster ripped my throat open and robbed me of my life. Now, I am nothing. Now, I am no one. I forget once again.

Until   I   remember.

Chapter Two

I was murdered. A hideous monster killed me.

Not just me. There were so many broken bodies. There was so much blood coating the pristine floors of my home. The screams; I can still hear the screams. Why can I still hear the screams? I open my mouth to speak, but I can't. I don't remember how.

Why can't I?

I'm floating in this endless space. There is no wind, there is no cold, no heat, it just is. A vacuum of endless confusion. The screams. Where am I? Why are there screams? I try to awaken from this dream, but there is no shift in my consciousness. I forget again why I'm here. I forget who I am as if my memories have gotten lost in a storm.

Then, as quickly as I forget, I remember. My name. My name is Jasmine. Jasmine Marie Whitmore. But, I died. I died on the floor of my parent's room, my throat cut open by a horrible monster. I ran as fast as I could. I punched in the code to the panic room, but I wasn't fast enough. The door didn't shut fast enough.

What was that thing? Why did it come for us? Why am I here? Who am I?

Jasmine. My name is Jasmine.

The cycle continues. I remember, and then I forget. I don't understand why I keep forgetting. Is it the trauma or is it my punishment, doomed to rewind and hit play on the tragedy that was my death? Maybe the afterlife is not so kind after all. Maybe we all must suffer for eternity. And that's just what it seems to be. Floating in a void, not quite awake, not quite unconscious. Forgetting and then remembering, unable to completely recall my life.

I fight to remember, afraid my memories will fade if I don't. I had a family. I had a mom, dad, and a big sister. Elizabeth, Jason, and-. I forget. I had a sister. Her name was Rayne. I called her. I warned her. I wanted to protect my sister. Tell her that it wasn't safe to come home. My sister never answered the phone, she never responded to my calls, never promised me that she was safe.

The movies. I wanted to go see one with her and then go shopping, but she spent the night at her friend's, no, her girlfriend's house. Selene's house. She stayed with Selene and never answered the phone. I texted her over and over hoping to annoy her for fun like a good little sister does, but she didn't answer. I didn't think to call Selene's phone. By then, there was no time left.

One of the men that worked security rushed through the door. He slammed it so hard that it popped back open. He closed it again, back pressed against the wood, and turned to face me and the housekeepers. He was short and well built, his black suit stretched over his defined muscles. There was sweat matting his short black hair. His eyes were wide as saucers and he had blood dripping down his brow. His mouth was opening and closing like a fish left on land to die. I had made the trip down the stairs to look for a snack, but I pulled up short once I saw the guard.

"Dad?" I called hesitantly.

The housekeepers and I stood there like a detective without a clue. I pulled the headphones from my ear and looked around for my father. He came around the corner, probably from his office and stopped in the middle of the floor. Dad was tall, but not imposing, yet he still effortlessly drew your attention. Easily handsome with short, dark curly hair and dark brown intelligent eyes. His dress shirt was untucked and wrinkled. There's stubble growing back on his chin, making him look older than he normally does, more rugged. His mouth was pressed in a thin line, making his full lips seem smaller. He scanned the scene and immediately realized that something was amiss.

"Lee, what's going on out there? Are you okay?" my father asked, hand out, stepping forward, ready to react to anything that may be wrong. He kept walking until he was in front of me, even if he was a distance away.

My mom must have heard the wariness in his voice because she came out of the kitchen wiping her hands on a paper towel. "Jason? Is everything alright?"

She was wearing a black sleeveless blouse with dark blue jeans. Her long brunette hair was pulled back into a messy ponytail and her normally bright hazel eyes were dark with worry. She could easily see the look of distress on Lee's face.

The lights flickered. The housekeepers mumbled something under their breath about a fuse, but the way Lee was still paralyzed with fear made me feel that it wasn't a fuse at all.

"Lee? What's happening?" My father asked again, more firmly. It was the voice he used in his business dealings.

Then, the screams began as something huge and powerful slammed into the front door causing the wood trim to become loose.

My memory fades again and I can't help but shiver even if there's no wind. The terror that I experienced may have splintered my memory, but the primal part of me hasn't forgotten. Even if I can barely remember my name.

Jasmine. Jazzy. Rayne calls me Jazzy.

My name is Jasmine Whitmore. I am thirteen years old. I have an older sister named Rayne and I love to paint. My parents are...

Light explodes all around me, so bright that even as I try to cover my eyes, it is so blinding that it's like I'm standing in front of the sun and looking directly into it. My eyes burn and tears fall like rain.

How am I crying if I'm dead? How am I feeling pain and fear?

The brightness recedes until the world is illuminated by light like that of a street lamp. I can see directly in front of me, but anything in the distance is still blanketed in darkness. There is still no warmth, nor cold. Yet, I shiver again. If I died, then what about my parents? My mom. Shouldn't I at least be with her? I don't think she made it.

Her screams echo in the back of my mind.

I try to focus, to will the memory back to me, but it doesn't work. I frown and I squint, attempting with all my might to recall, but anguish fills me. It's a tornado in my belly. I can barely remember what she looks like. How long have I been here, floating into nothingness?

How long does it take to forget the face of your mother?

I fall to my knees, inhale as much air as I can into my lungs, and scream as loud as I can manage. Surprisingly, sound comes out, but it's sucked up into the darkness. I'm in a vacuum. It's silenced as quickly as I release it. The scream makes me feel better, alive even. Though I know that it can't be possible. After what happened to me... No, no one could survive that.

What did I do wrong to earn this type of afterlife? To be trapped in my own personal hell all alone forever. I just want to give up, curl into a ball and fade away into nothingness.

Chapter Three

I'm a Whitmore. That much I remember. We don't give up. We don't cry in a corner when things get rough. Someone I love very much told me that. They taught me a lot.

I must start moving. I won't find answers if I stay here.

I begin to walk and it's like I am suddenly propelled forward as the entire world shifts. I might as well be in a racecar speeding down the track as fast as the landscape changes before me. Then, I'm hit with agonizing pain as my memories melt back into my brain with the heat of third degree burns. I remember everything. All the pain that I endured before my death, all my fear, every single impression seems to overload my mind. I put my hands on the sides of my head and scream until my throat is raw.

I am being rebuilt. I am a jigsaw puzzle of emotions and sensations.

I stop screaming as my mind settles back into a normal state. The chill in the air eats at me. The throbbing in my head continues. The cold pounds against my flesh, worsening my aches. It feels like it's settling in my bones.

I force my eyes to open as I survey the landscape. There is nothing staring back at me but stone, dirt, and scarce foliage. The wind howls as it blows the dust around me. I'm forced to cover my face with my arm as I try unsuccessfully to keep the dust out of my mouth. I manage to cough and spit up most of it, but there's nothing I can do for the chill that has burrowed its way into me.

I force myself to begin moving again as the wind slightly settles. Gripping onto any tree, bush, or boulder I can find, I begin a steady pace. I wish I had a pair of my designer sunglasses right about now to keep the grit from my eyes. But, I guess there are no such luxuries for the dead.

After what seems like an eternity, I finally see a figure off in the distance. I trip on a few rocks in excitement, the wind keeping me off balance. Ignoring the pain in my hands from the jagged stones scraping against my palms, I pop up, waving frantically.

"Hey! Hey, over here!"

They turn and I smile at being able to get their attention. But, they make no move toward me. Maybe they can't see me through the flying debris.

"Hey, I need your help!" I call, louder this time. "I'm lost!"

This time, they begin to move, leaping over rocks with inhuman speed. A wave of fear hits me as I remember the thing that killed me. It's the same type of feeling. It's as if I've been punched in the gut and am trying to hold down my vomit. I back up fearfully, looking around for somewhere to hide. I steal another glance at the thing now coming after me. Everything about it screams "wrong."

Jagged, sharp teeth that are experts at ripping flesh apart are flashing me, lips pulled back in a snarl It has pupil-less eyes, slits for a nose, "u" shaped horns growing on its forehead, cloven feet, and claws on its hands. I'll never be able to outrun this thing. It gallops as skillfully as a stallion across the uneven terrain. I've already died once, I don't want to know what will happen if I get taken this time.

The monster leaps at me and I fall flat to the ground, grabbing a rock bigger than my small hand in the process. It readjusts itself after its first miss and spins in a cloud of dust. I grip the rock tighter and swing, just as it leaps at me again. The monster howls in rage as I connect with the side of its head. I get up as quickly as I can in an attempt to put as much distance between me and my attacker. The rock still remains in my grip.

I try to ignore the wind and chill as it picks up, but I can't ignore how the hair on the back of my neck stands. It's instinct, primal. I don't need to look around to know that I'm being surrounded. The growls from behind me are enough.

I'm going to need a bigger rock.

Two of them leap at once. I duck down and cover my face as I hear the slam of bodies colliding. The monsters scramble to untangle themselves. Jaws snap so close to my face that I can smell the stench of rotted meat between its teeth. Then, all I feel is heat. When I open my eyes, a tall figure stands next to me with a flaming sword in his hand. The inferno burns bright and uncomfortably hot. None of the creatures dare to attempt to penetrate the thick, six feet wall of flame. The ring of fire separates us from the rest of the monsters and one in front of me is disappearing in a black wisp of smoke.

"I'm sorry, Jasmine. The fault lies with me. You should have never been attacked. I was careless." He reaches out his hand, but never turns his gaze from the enemies. Even if he can control fire, he's not taking any chances. "I'm here now to protect you. Take my hand."

I look up at the man, but he isn't a man at all. He's about seventeen; skin the same light brown complexion as mine, long, brown hair braided into a ponytail, tattoos covering his shirtless chest and back. The sword is still feeding the hungry blaze. His black pants are rolled up to reach his ankles and he's not wearing any shoes. He looks more trustworthy than the things trying to kill me, even if he's flooding. At least he knows my name.

I grab his hand. It's large, warm, and comforting. In seconds, he pulls me up and wraps his arm around my waist. It startles me as my face crushes against his smooth chest. He smells of fire and ash. I don't have time to pull away because he tears through reality like I'm in a racecar as the world zooms by. When he releases me, I fall back to the ground, dry heaving from overwhelming dizziness and nausea that seems to have a personal vendetta against me.

He helps me back up slowly with features soft with worry. Satisfied that I am uninjured, he releases me and his sword disappears. I step back instinctively, not really knowing if he's a different type of threat to me. He may have saved me, but he did say that it was his fault I was in the situation in the first place. It's not like I have anywhere to run if he turns on me.

"Forgive me, Jasmine," he says, reading my hesitation with his kind brown eyes. He tries to smile, his small lips covering his gums. Two rows of straight, white teeth shine at me. "My name is Micah and I am your soul guide."

"Uhhh. O-Kay." I look at my surroundings. It's warmer, brighter. The trees aren't just tall; they're the NBA players of trees. They're just as wide. It would take me twenty seconds just to walk around one. The green of the leaves is a mix of lime, forest, mint, olive, chartreuse, and emerald. The ground is covered in thick shamrock colored grass and shrubbery every color of the rainbow. It's all extraordinarily vibrant as if colored with a fresh box of paint. The land around us is alive.

The ground breathes energy. I don't know how I know this, but it's true. I have no doubt. It wants to give something to us. It wants to protect us.

This place feels strangely like home.

"What is a soul guide? No, what is this place? Am I dead for real or in a weird limbo type-thing?" I shake my head as I try to go through all the questions that I have.

"How about I just start at the beginning?" He chuckles and reaches for my hand again. "Come, let's have a seat." Micah leads me to a garden with beautiful, vivid, asters, azaleas, begonias, crocuses, lavender, a three-tiered fountain, and a light gray soapstone bench that's much more comfortable than it looks. Though I'm beginning to suspect that nothing is what it seems.

It's eerie how soothing it feels to be right here right now. I frown in confusion. In the distance, through the trees, I can make out a large building shining proudly against the sunlight. I can worry about that later. Now, I just focus my attention on the person in front of me. He's still standing, arms crossed and eyes constantly scanning as if he's standing guard. Maybe he is. He may be young, but he carries himself like a soldier.

"So... About all of this? Yeah," I say, looking around and gesturing.

"Okay. Once again, Jasmine, my name is Micah, and I am your soul guide." He bows low. "I was chosen to act as your mentor and protector. You were destined to become like me, a soul tamer. Do you understand so far?"

"Uhh, no. I understand the concept of destiny just fine. But to me it sounds like you're saying that it was predetermined for me to end up here with you. How? Why? Destiny, soul tamer, death, with me caught in the middle. Is this limbo or is this just how death is for everyone? Maybe I'm not ready to learn what's going on." I stand up and try to brush past him, not knowing which way to go. Surprisingly, Micah doesn't follow. He allows me to go. My pulse pounds in my ears and if I had time to think on how crazy it is that I feel a pulse, I would probably freak out. Soon, I sit back down, face in my hands.

"Death is but another transition into another existence. You are dead, but you have a new kind of life as well. I'll try to explain as best I can. There are gifts from life that you were allowed to hold onto. You still feel your heart beat, fear, happiness, surprise. You still sweat, cry, feel love, and pain. It is a gift for the life you've given up."

"A gift? It sounds like something a business would pay a client they screwed over. Hush money for sealing my fate."

"Jasmine, only upon death was your fate predetermined. Well, you were meant to die later, but circumstances changed and you were called home sooner. I am sorry for that, but you are home now and you have a destiny to fulfill. You are a soul tamer. I will mold you into a great one," he says proudly.

I just sit there letting his words sink in. Finally, I take a deep breath, forcing back tears. "So, I died, I had to go through all of that, because you needed me? I had my throat ripped open. My family was brutalized! Was all that to get to me?" I feel like I can't breathe. It's almost funny. As if I need air now.

"No. Those circumstances are their own. I just know that it was only your life that we intervened in. I'm sorry." He has the decency to hang his head in shame.

"You're sorry? I'm dead! My dreams, everything that I wanted to do, all the things that I wanted to experience, I can't. And you think I'm going to just help you? Send me back." I have to keep myself from throwing the world's greatest tantrum, even if it is justified.

"I can't, I'm sorry, more than you know. But it is the trauma of our deaths that sends us here. I was drowned by my best friend. I understand your pain. I know what you went through, but believe me, what we do here is more important than our lives that we lived."

"I am thirteen, Micah. I didn't ask for this," I cry. My tears feel heavy with my burden.

"Neither did I, Jasmine, but I learned to accept it."

"And if I don't?" I ask defiantly.

"We will give you some time, but you will. It is in you. It's who you are, who you've always been."

"How can you be so sure? I'm not any more special than anyone else."

"You are more special than you know." He smiles sadly. "If you weren't, they would have never done what they did to you."

"Who are they?" I ask quietly. I want to speak with them.

"The Soul Kings. They are chosen among the angels and select those of us with divine qualities to become soul tamers. We don't see them, ever, but they speak to us."

"Why are they different than other angels? How do they speak to you?"

"That, I do not know. No one does. But, they send messages through our minds. They either give us visual messages or they speak to us."

"Well, what is a soul tamer? Why are we so important?"

"Think of us as foot soldiers for the army of good vs. evil. Angels can't be everywhere and do everything regardless of what you believe. They are the last defense especially if there is an apocalypse. Soul tamers are more hands on. We're humans that possess the power to keep the world in balance. We have numerous jobs, but we mainly keep souls from being taken and devoured by demons. Sometimes, we're obligated to keep souls from escaping their prisons, and sometimes we're able to help souls move on. We have plenty of jobs to do and the good part is if you serve honorably, you can be reincarnated to live life again, if you so choose."

"How long does that take?"

He remains silent for a few seconds too long.

"Let me guess, forever." I laugh and shake my head. I must be going crazy. There's no way that this is really happening. I'm being pranked. Ashton? Where's Ashton Kutcher?

"I don't have the answer. It's different for everyone."

"That's because the Soul Kings give you something to look forward to and never follow through on it."

"That's not true. They are fair."

"They killed me so I can serve them."

Slavery.

"You are more valuable here. You will save countless people." His voice is urgent like I must hurry to believe. I need to see what he sees. It's a matter of... life and death.

"Kill me to save hundreds."

"No, Jasmine. Kill you to save millions."

I narrow my eyes. "What do you mean?"

He sighs. "That is a conversation for later. We have the power to tune our soul's resonance to another in order to find souls anywhere. Think of it like playing the same song on the same radio frequency. Only soul tamers have that power. It's just a small part of what the Soul Kings have given us. We can even find souls in the mortal world. Sometimes souls need help passing on or assistance in getting to their final place of rest here in this world. I will teach you. I need to apologize again for my carelessness. There was a soul in need right before your passing. I was supposed to be there to assist you during your transition, but I took too long. In your confusion, you began to travel to other planes, which are other destinations in the otherworld. There may have been another soul there that you were drawn to. I've never seen that happen and I didn't feel another soul when I came to get you. The demons could have devoured it."

I try not to think about anything devouring a soul. "So, if I'm able to find souls, I can find my parents and sister?" I get up and begin pacing.

Micah shakes his head. "Your sister lives. You will not be able to tune your soul to hers. You can't see her or your parents. It is forbidden."

"Why? Isn't it the least they can do, after everything that was taken from me?" I clench my fists in anger, digging my nails into my hands. If I could draw blood, I would.

"I agree with you. Jasmine, but in order to do our jobs, we must cut all ties. We'd never be able to move on otherwise. I'm sorry."

"You sure are doing a lot of apologizing, Micah. It's not as if you came up with the rules."

"I know, and I know this is hard for you, that's why we will give you some time to adjust. You are safe here. Maybe in time, you will be allowed to look in on your sister, but you can't interact. It seems that the call that you placed to her caused her to go to your house to investigate. She and her lover were attacked."

The wind picks up and blows my hair into my eyes, but I ignore it as I freak out. "Oh, my God. Is she okay? Did she see our bodies?" She may not be dead, but she could be seriously injured. How will she be able to deal with all our deaths? Rayne. My heart breaks for my big sister and the pieces are too small to reattach.

"Her witch was able to protect her. She is injured, but they are safe, for now. She has been in and out of consciousness."

"Witch? What are you talking about?"

"Her lover, Selene, is it; she is witch born, a powerful one at that. There is much hope for her; even here, her potential is praised." He waves a hand in front of my face and an image of Selene's outstretched hands protecting Rayne with a burst of magic flickers before my eyes. It's gone too soon for me to even process everything.

They were in my parent's room which means that they did see my body. Rayne looked frightened, but there was something else in her eyes. Determination. Maybe she will be okay.

I close my eyes and try to center myself.

"Let's take a step back. How can Selene be a witch? What does that really mean?"

"You have much to learn." He chuckles and closes his eyes. After a few seconds, he's dressed in dark jeans and a t-shirt. My eyes go wide and he laughs again. It's a laugh full of joy and it's contagious.

I can't help but to laugh too, even if I don't understand why.

"The world of awakeneds is vast and mind blowing. Those of us that were born human are but a small group that walk the earth. We share the world with witches, werewolves, vampires, demons, the fae, and more. Soul tamers can only be human and they are chosen by the Soul Kings the minute they are conceived. We are born with a divine spark. We are different on a spiritual level."

"So, you mean to tell me that I've been living among monsters the whole time? My sister is dating a witch? Selene's a witch. If Rayne knew and didn't tell me, I'm gonna..."

Micah looks at me humorously waiting for me to finish my empty threat.

"I'll haunt her. I don't know." My brain explodes. "That is so cool." And, how did you do the clothes thing?"

"All in time. I think that's enough for now. You should take a look around at your new home. I'll show you to your quarters first, and then you can explore."

"It's not like I have anywhere else to go." I pause, look into Micah's eyes, and hope that he's as honest as I think he is. "Are you sure that Rayne's alright?"

He smiles patiently at me again. Then, he closes his eyes. "I promise that your sister is safe at the present time. That is all I can offer you."

"Okay. Thank you. She's all I have left." I'll just have to take what I can get for now.

Micah nods in understanding. "I recognize the need to protect your family. I was the middle child. I left behind two brothers. I was close with both of them and knowing I had to leave them behind was incredibly devastating. None of us had it especially easy growing up and we all relied on each other's strength."

"I'm sorry."

"Look who's doing the apologizing now." He smiles sadly. "It's alright. They are both old men and I have plenty of nieces and nephews to look in on now. It was fifty years ago. I'm happy that they were able to live full lives."

"You've been doing this for fifty years? When do you go on vacation?"

"I have certain privileges. Some of us have been at this for hundreds of years. But again, you can learn about this later. Let me take you to your home."

I agree and stand up to follow Micah down a long path that winds through the garden that we're sitting in. The walkway is made up of octagon shaped precious moonstones that reflect the sky and light around it. Each stone is two feet wide and spaced a foot away from the next with perfectly manicured grass between. We cross a small bridge over a creek and past a group of people that are quietly meditating on some rocks as the water runs past them in a small pond. They don't stir as we walk past. We keep following the path and the sense of home gets even stronger. I can finally make out the building that I saw in the distance.

There isn't just one building, but a cluster of structures, sort of like an apartment complex. Each building is "u" shaped. In between the arms of the "u" design and surrounding each structure is a courtyard with perfectly paved pathways of rubies, amethyst, sapphires, and citrine gems accented with cherry blossom and wisteria trees, and neatly trimmed rose bushes, other shrubs, fountains, benches, koi ponds, and a gazebo with seating. The area takes up half a football field in length.

It looks like a high-end resort. It's a spa trip for the afterlife. All it's missing is cabana boys fanning you with huge leaves and drinks with pineapples and umbrellas sticking out the glass. I'm sure there's probably a hot spring around here somewhere. I must admit, it's all jaw droppingly beautiful.

The buildings are so white that they brilliantly shine as if there is stardust coating the smooth walls. There are three buildings total and eight floors in each.

Micah walks me to the one on the left. "These are the dormitories for the soul tamers in training. You will live here for about five years and then you will move to permanent quarters of your choosing. There are plenty of places in this world for you to pick. I'm sure you'll eventually find a place to your liking."

We follow the immaculate stone path until we're about twenty feet away from three doors in front of each section of the building. Each door depicts an angel. It's beautiful, the artwork so lifelike.

The first angel is kneeling, head down as if awaiting orders. His brilliant, glittering, gold wings are outstretched and impossibly long. The next angel seems to stare right at me with knowing eyes, a helmet that splits his face down the middle and a long sword in one hand. The last angel is female with flowing hair.

She has one knee in the air, her chin lifted toward the sky with wings up as if getting ready to take off with a burst of air.

"The door is a seal. Only those that are chosen can enter. The angel will shimmer and disappear for you to cross the threshold. You will always be safe here." He gestures to the design of the building. You will share the dorms with twenty others, but your quarters are your own. Every floor belongs to just one person. Based on the design, you can see that the building is separated into three sections."

"One entire floor is ours. Three sections in this "u" designed apartment building. Twenty-one of us live here. Enter via the angels. That's it?"

"Correct." He puts a hand on the small of my back and leads me in the building. "Now, you are on the sixth floor." He walks me toward the kneeling angel. I guess this is my stop. As soon as we're two feet from the door, as Micah stated, the angel shimmers and then disappears, granting us entry into a vast opening with walls completely covered in portraits. I'll have to explore later.

On the wall closest to us, there are gold numbers that buzz with energy. I run my hand over the number six, prepared to ask how it creates the pulsing energy when in a shimmering haze, Micah and I are now standing in a room next to a white chaise lounge, a paint easel facing the window, a canopy bed with red and white throw pillows, a bookshelf, and training equipment such as staffs, punching bags, sharp weapons I couldn't even begin to name, and targets on the other side. I turn to Micah in question.

"This is your room. When you touch the numbers below, you are transported to your destination. It's much easier since this is your space, but for others, it takes a little more thought. There are no elevators or stairs."

I look around once again. The ceiling is fifteen feet tall and the rest of the room is a perfect square. It's about forty feet by forty feet. There are also some things that look identical to my room back home like my white vanity, flower wall decals, long mirror, and my bamboo panel room divider. But my eyes stop on the blank canvas and unopened paints on the floor. Micah puts a hand on my shoulder.

"I heard that you love to paint. I wanted you to at least be able to do that."

Tears well up in my eyes, but I blink them away. "Thank you for that."

"Whatever I'm able to do, I will try. Now, if there is nothing else, I will leave you. When you are ready to leave, just imagine the front door again with the intent of being there, and you will be transported. When you are ready, think of me, and I will come. You have some reading material as well and you are free to explore as you please. Remember, you are not a prisoner. This is your home."

I nod. "How much time will you give me?"

"As much as you need. I really am sorry, Jasmine Whitmore. I hope that one day, you will come to understand why this had to happen." Then, he disappears in a glow of gold light.

Once I'm sure that I'm alone, I walk to the window and allow my tears to fall with no restraint.

Chapter Four

I don't know how long I lie on the floor, curled up into a ball, but the tears have long stopped flowing. The complicated mixture of my emotions has worn me completely out. It's been a roller coaster and now I'm just left feeling sick. But, there is no medicine to cure this pain.

First, I cried for myself. I mourned for all that I endured. I remembered all the pain and fear to the point that I was overwhelmed with nausea. The slice of claws tearing through my flesh, digging into my insides. Burning, searing agony. Darkness, darkness, death.

I screamed and threw a tantrum for all that I had lost, what I would never again get to do, and what I would never experience. It hurt as if my heart had been brutally ripped from my chest, the ache still too vivid. Death is supposed to bring peace.

This isn't peace.

I miss my parents already and the thought of never seeing them again hurts me to my very soul. Their sacrifices bring me pride as well as rage. I can't help but think that it's partly my fault, that my "needing" to die caused their deaths. How do I get over that?

Tears of joy fall for my sister. We may be gone, but she gets to live. She'll find a way to push through the pain and survive. It's who she is. Rayne possesses a fire that I've always been envious of. She was always the strong one. I just hope that she never forgets us, that she never forgets me.

◊◊◊

The gunshots do nothing to drown out the screams. Panic is in full swing as more men on dad's security team rush inside. There aren't too many that work this time of evening. They try to usher the last of the workers out the back but the words, "we're trapped," and "the door won't open," are echoed through the hallway. The lights flicker again, this time completely going out. Cursing and gunshots. Screams and gurgles. Slams, thuds, crashes, and cracks of bones and furniture breaking touch my ears. A foul stench of rot, blood, and death overwhelm my senses. My eyes burn and my stomach heaves. All of this takes less than a minute as I stand there frozen.

"Elizabeth, Jasmine, run!" my dad demands.

My mom frantically pushes me up the stairs, my phone nearly falling out of my hand. I pull my earphones out in the process. They tangle around my leg and I kick them away. I hadn't realized that I was clutching the device so tightly that my hand begins to cramp as I stumble. My mom steadies me.

My father dictates behind us as he yells for a gun. He tells his men to stand their ground, but soon his own voice is cut off in mid-sentence. Glass breaks behind me and I start to turn my head, but my mom's hand on my shoulder turns me back around.

"We have to go to the panic room." There's a loud set of booming footsteps behind us. I hear my mom turn and gasp. She speaks quickly, turning back to me, looking me in the eyes with all the love that she can muster. Even in the dark, her brilliant hazel eyes shine.

She tries to mask the fear in her gaze, but it's impossible to miss, like I'm standing in front of a mountain. She touches my cheek and begins to cry. I stare at her heart-shaped face, perfectly threaded eyebrows, button nose, small lips, and dimples. "I love you, my little, beautful girl. So much. You remember the code, don't you?' I nod. She says it anyway, "Nine, five, seven, three, three, zero, eight."

"Nine, five, seven, three, three, zero, eight," I repeat dutifully.

"Go." She pushes me so hard toward her room that I nearly fall. I watch her pull a painting off the wall. It's the only weapon around. "Jazzy, go!"

I run to the room as I hear my mother scream like a warrior going into battle. It sends shivers up my spine. Her footsteps echo into the night and in the back of my mind, I know that I'll never see her again. I shut the thought away just as I shut the door to my parent's bedroom with my hands shaking and my heart running a marathon.

First, I try to barricade the door, but the nearby dresser is too heavy and too far. I give up; try to ignore the horrible sounds coming from the other side, and run to the far wall, trying to feel for the panel to the panic room. I find it, rip the small part open where the security console is, and fumble as I punch in the buttons. It takes three tries in my nervousness to finger the right code.

The door matches the light gray of the walls. It opens with a swoosh and I have to step back as the heavy steel swings toward me. I look at my phone and a tiny sliver of a bar pops up. I hit the button to shut the door as I call to warn my sister. She had ignored all my other pestering calls and texts, but I hope that this one is received.

The call goes straight to voicemail and I hit the number to hear the beep sooner. The door to my parent's room splinters into thousands of pieces. I try to speak quickly as the panic room door is finished closing. "Rayne, don't come home, something's..." The door doesn't shut; it's ripped right off the hinges. I scream as I'm pulled from the panic room, claws burying into my flesh. I throw my phone at my attacker's face and it shatters. Darkness seems to wrap around the thing holding me, giving me but a glimpse. But what I do see nearly kills me from fright. There are three mouths, tongues flicking, saliva dripping. It has no eyeballs, just empty holes that seem to try to suck me in. I try to block it out, but I grow weaker by the second. I kick and flail, falling on my back onto the floor.

My breath comes out of me with a whoosh and I roll to my stomach trying to crawl away, to get somewhere, anywhere, but the thing grabs my legs. I try to grip the carpet. Tears pour from my eyes as I'm dragged so hard my nails bleed. It lifts me up and throws me into a dresser.

Pain explodes through my whole body as if someone lit a fuse of dynamite under my flesh. It disorients me and the next thing I know is that I'm being grabbed once again by that vile thing. I have no fight in me. There's nothing left for me to do and I know that it's over. I give up. Brutally, the monster takes my life.

◊◊◊

The memory is burned into my soul, the knowledge that I could have lived, the door *should have* shut makes it even harder to bear. Someone, some divine type being intervened in my life and caused that to happen. They decided that there was a perfect opportunity for me to die. My mom sacrificed herself for nothing. If I was meant to die anyway, I should have sacrificed myself for her instead. She should have gone into the panic room. I should have stayed in the hallway. At least then, my sister wouldn't be alone.

So, what now?

This decision I'm supposed to make, this "divine calling" that's supposed to make all of this mean something is meant to be ingrained in me. There's only bitterness and resentment festering within. I didn't ask for this. There's no comfort for me even in this beautiful world. I might as well be on an iceberg in the middle of the ocean.

◊◊◊

Time may not really have much meaning anymore, but somehow, I can still sense it. It's been two days since I've been outside. I've noticed that it gets dark enough to be considered late evening, but that's it. There's no veil of darkness like only midnight to four a.m. can bring. I've watched the brightness of day dim slowly before re-brightening about six hours later.

Micah's kept his promise of leaving me alone. No one has appeared out of nowhere to bother me. Nobody has demanded that I snap out of this funk that I'm in. For that, I'm grateful. I think it's time to at least see what the world has to offer. I can't stay in this room for eternity.

I imagine that beautifully intricate front door, the magnificent angel genuflecting and am placed at the front. I admit, it's pretty awesome. The air is the perfect temperature where pants aren't uncomfortable and shorts won't make you chilly. I immediately adjust to the brightness and vibrancy of this world.

The sky is a bold mixture of blues. It's a deep lapis in the distance, and nearly ice blue closer to where I am. The earth seems even more colorful than before as if covered in a fresh coat of paint. The flora bathe the air in a sweet, intimate scent of home. It's a smell that you recognize as belonging to something of yours. Even the small breeze seems to caress my skin as if it means to comfort.

For a few minutes, I just take the time to enjoy everything that pleases my senses and look around, scanning the area, trying to figure out where I'm going to go. I decide to follow the path opposite my window. It winds around the dorm into an area that I haven't been able to see.

The path takes me to a bunch of hills spotted with trees and other growth. I break from the paved walkway and step into the soft, impossibly green grass. Colors like this don't exist in the mortal world. Or, maybe I just didn't have the ability to see it for what it is. Maybe, I should have tried to appreciate the feel of the grass, the color of the sky more.

Maybe.

But, it's too late for that.

I climb higher to the peak of a hill and sigh. My emotions are boiling over, but even I can admit that this is peaceful and beautiful. On one side of the hills is a vast forest and directly in front of me in the distance are more buildings like my dorm and the landscaping that surrounds my new home. In between the hills and the other housing is a lake with black sand contrasting against the crystal blue water that reflects the light like millions of diamonds on the surface.

I wish Rayne could see this. She loves to be near the water.

I plop down, run my hand through my short auburn hair, and then wrap my arms around my knees. I'm still wearing the white sleeveless blouse, purple high waisted shorts, and purple and white sandals that I died in and it just makes me think of home all over again.

I close my eyes and will my spirit to reach out and touch my sister to let her know that it's okay. I try really hard, but nothing happens. I didn't expect it to. I just know that she'll take my death the hardest. She'll find a way to blame herself. God, I hope that Selene can keep her sane.

Time ticks by and I end up on my back, arms stretched out, staring at the sky. It takes all my energy to not scream into the air. Instead, I ask, "Micah, who killed me, and why?"

Micah bleeds into existence, sitting next to me with his knees to his chest. He has on a black tank top and gray sweat pants. His long ponytail rocks gently against his back. The warrior stares ahead, thinking of how to answer my inquiry.

"I'm trying to give the most simple, clear answer. The demon, the devourer, a foul beast may have committed the act, but a witch by the name of Namen Young is who summoned the demon. The motivation was revenge. Your father had something that he wanted. Weapons, I believe." Micah finally turns to me and gives a sad smile.

"There's more, isn't there?"

"Yes. Your father retaliated against Namen after he kidnapped and killed some of your father's employees."

My eyes narrow. "Retaliated how?"

"He kidnapped and killed one of Namen's men. Our belief is that Namen hoped that your father would do just that. He was known for reacting that way. Your father was a good man, but he was not without his sins. He could be brutal when he felt justified."

"That's why the opportunity for my death arose? Because that demon had come to kill my dad? He set all of this in motion." My dad. The perfect father. Not so much. Not at all.

Micah responds to my questions, but I ignore him. My head is spinning around. I feel like I'm trapped in a hamster wheel that's going one hundred mph. It makes me sick. I can't think about it too much and keep my sanity.

I just can't.

"Can all witches summon demons? Is Rayne really safe?" A subject change makes me feel one thousand times better.

He's a fast study. "Fear not. The witch, Selene will keep your sister safe. Some witches can indeed summon demons. Anyone with the proper knowledge can do it, but they often pay with their lives or souls."

"What's going to happen to my dad?"

"That, I cannot say. It is more complicated than you will understand and more complex than any religion can adequately explain. It is just not my place to speak on. I'm sorry."

"It's not your fault. Thank you for telling me. Now, I have to process hearing that my dad killed people. I mean, I knew he used to be a drug dealer before he went to the military, but he never acted like he killed people." Not that I know how murderers are supposed to act.

"I don't know what to tell you. I don't have all the answers, but I'll be here for support when you need me. Many of us have done things that we aren't proud of, but that doesn't mean that we aren't redeemable. You want to know why we feel emotions and pain here, even in death?"

"Sure."

"Just like we must suffer to reach this place, we can't ever be turned off from our human emotions because we'd lose sight of why we fight. The more human we remain, the more powerful our urge to protect the souls from demons, dark spirits, or whatever else may come our way."

"We fight for humanity, so we get to keep ours. It's a balance," I say in understanding.

"We?" he asks, hopeful.

"I don't know. Maybe."

"Sometimes, we train in teams of four. Would you like to meet the other three and their guides? You can hear their stories if they're willing to share. Maybe then, at the very least, you'll see that you're not alone."

"Sure. It's not like I have somewhere else to be. Are they my age?"

"For the most part. You are the youngest that we've had in a long while. All soul tamers pass on before thirty. Our powers are the strongest within our age range. There are a lot of factors that come into play. Young people are often more sensitive to the supernatural. It slips away as we become jaded to the bad things we witness in the world. There's something powerful about the soul of someone young. Our lives, our deaths. There is strength in each. It's almost as if the future can only be protected by those who no longer have one."

"So, what if I had died later, like if I was eighteen or nineteen; would I be stronger?"

"No. It's just that after thirty years, our powers diminish. You are born with your strength at its fullest. It just doesn't manifest itself until we reach puberty and then pass on. You, Jasmine are tremendously strong. You already traveled to another world without much of a thought."

"So, am I stronger than the others?"

"That remains to be seen. I do not know the entire reason why you are so important, just that the time will come when we will all need you."

"That's a heavy burden for someone as young as I, don't you think."

"There once were kings your age. Do not doubt yourself. They had help and so will you. You are kind, smart, talented, and you are worthy enough to walk in this world. Burdens are meant to test us. I will not let you fail."

"You sound so sure."

"I can be nothing else."

"Why?"

"Because I believe it."

Micah stares me down with such intensity that I instinctively back up. If I was still alive, I'd think that look was attraction. Here, I know that it's his passion from his desire to help me. Still, it's scary and a little uncomfortable. He notices my demeanor change and looks away.

"How old are you, Micah? Well, how old were you when you died?"

"Seventeen. It was a week after my birthday, actually. My best friend had started to hang out with a group of white boys that didn't like me, even though both of my parents were biracial. Couples like them were very rare. One day, I'll tell you about both of their stories and how they met. Interracial marriage was illegal back then, so I'm sure you can understand how they felt about biracial children. Anyway, he... my friend, let them get to him. They told him that he needed to play a little prank on me. We all went down to the local creek, got drunk, and were jumping in."

Micah pauses as he remembers, but puts a small smile on his face as if what he's about to tell me isn't a big deal. But, I know that it is, no matter how long he's had to get over it. Being murdered by your best friend is something that would be probably one of the most horrible ways to go.

I hadn't even thought about my best friend, Tiffany at all. She's probably hurting so bad too. I didn't even take her feelings into account. Some friend I am. All I've thought about was how my family felt, but I had friends too. They knew my secrets. We had sleepovers together. We talked every single day about everything and nothing, yet it took Micah to tell me about his friend's betrayal to even have her cross my mind.

I feel ashamed. Tiffany is loud and goofy. She does whatever she can to keep everyone around her smiling without being overly obnoxious. Oh, she has her annoying moments, but as a friend, she's the best. She gets even more excited about good news than the person it happens to. She cries during Disney movies and when we watch "The Notebook." I wonder who's there to comfort my friend that always does the comforting. There's probably something broken inside of her now too.

Micah continues, not sensing my inner turmoil. "We all started betting to see who could hold their breath the longest. I'd done it a million times. But, when I pulled up out of the water, I stared right at him with a smile and he hit me in the head with a rock and I went back under. They all laughed. The sound was clear to me even under water. Blood poured into my eyes and I couldn't see when I came back up for air. But, I heard them screaming at him to finish it. Everything seemed to slow down then. He told them he didn't want to. I was already pretty out of it and I remember grabbing his arm, begging for him to help me out of the water. I wiped the blood out of the way and I'll never forget his expression. He just looked at me with disgust like it was my fault that we were in this situation. They told him to finish it or they'd kill us both."

"And he believed them."

"Yes, he did. I fought him off, but he was always stronger than me and on the wrestling team. I kept going under. I was drunk and wounded so the blood poured more freely. He choked me and I fought as hard as I could, beating against his chest, clawing at his eyes, but everything was so slippery. He was crying the entire time, begging me to forgive him. I remember staring up at him through the water, his eyes were dead. He looked nothing like my best friend."

"That is horrible." I crash into him and wrap my arms around his long torso. He's hesitant to return the embrace, but I squeeze harder. "I'm sorry that you had to go through that."

"It's okay. I serve a greater purpose now."

"But, that doesn't take away from what happened. You suffered. You're still suffering. How is that fair? It's certainly not okay to me."

Micah pulls away as if he's never thought about that before. "It's fair because we all suffer, Jasmine. I am not unique in that case. Who am I to think that I should be above that?"

"I didn't mean-,"

"No, you didn't, but it is what you said."

"I'm sorry."

He sighs and then smirks. "Look who's apologizing now."

"Whatever. I'm just saying. It kind of sucks that we have to be put through stuff like that, all for the greater good."

"Only those that understand true suffering can be true warriors for peace and balance."

"Empathy."

"Empathy."

"Fine. I get it. What happened to them?" I can't help but to ask.

"Well, the other boys tried to pin it all on my friend. He went to jail and committed suicide a year later. Then, one of the other boys finally confessed. I believe that they all served about twenty plus years."

"So, do you think that's justice?" I ask.

He looks surprised at my question and hesitant to answer, so I stop him with a hand in the air.

"Can we just go meet the others now? And let's not just zip there, how about we walk and enjoy the scenery."

"Sounds perfect."

Chapter Five

$\mathcal{A}$s we walk along the path, I slowly begin to feel like a transfer student on her first day. It's like the year has been started for months now and I'm going to be the awkward kid that no one knows. They'll have inside jokes and will already have their seats at the lunch table. I'll get picked last in gym and have to wait another year to try out for the dance team.

Okay, maybe I'm exaggerating because I've watched too many high school teen movies, but still. I will be the new kid. The young new kid and there's still a chance that they may not like me.

"What if they don't like me?" I voice aloud.

"It doesn't matter if they like you or not. You're only going to be around them for nearly eternity."

"Micah!"

He laughs. "They will like you. If they don't, they will learn to like you. It's not a big deal."

"So you say. Kids these days are brutal, okay. They can really be mean."

"Are you really worried about that? Have you ever not been popular?"

"No, and that's what I'm afraid of."

"Why have you always been popular?"

"Because, I'm nice to everyone, even the ones I probably shouldn't be nice to because they're not nice to anyone else. And, because I show interest in lots of things, stay involved in activities."

"Well, it's pretty much the same. Be nice and take interest in what we're doing here. Remember, these are the ones that will have your back. We all protect each other. They're going to want you to like them too."

"Fine."

He chuckles. "It will be."

We walk in silence, walking over a tiny wooden bridge that I had walked over when I first got here. Then, we go off to the right and trek through the growth until we reach a large outdoor meditation area. The structure was built around nature with vines and trees growing on and between the light blue walls. It reminds me of a Greek temple, high arches, open ceilings, and steps leading every which way.

Some parts also seem Buddhist in nature, with candles burning, rocks laid out in circular patterns, sand, pillows for seating, tiny pools of water, and an overpowering sense of peace. This is already going to be one of my favorite places.

It doesn't take us long to spot the group. They are up on the second level, seated in a circle. There are six of them and they all look up in unison as we climb the stairs and enter their quiet space. Micah puts a protective hand on my back and walks forward with me. I give everyone a smile and a small wave as they look me over curiously.

A tall, muscular man with thick, tight, curly, dark hair that reaches the top of his ears stands up first.

Everything about him says leader. He has a full goatee that's cut perfectly, a full mustache, thin line of hair under his lip, going into a beard that grows into his sideburns. He is handsome and equally intimidating. He looks as if he spent his entire life working in the sun. The permanent tint to his flesh makes me think that he was born somewhere near the desert. He's probably of Middle Eastern decent.

He eyes me the way a doctor evaluates a new patient. It's cold and impersonal. "So, The Eternal Flower has graced us with her presence. You are as beautiful as they say." He bows and I awkwardly try to bow back. It just ends up quick and jerky.

"How does she already have a nickname? None of us do." The speaker is pouting but he doesn't look like his heart is into it. There's a bit of mischief behind his eyes and I think I catch him wink at me with his stunning baby blues.

His hair is black, short, with loose curls, but somehow, he looks as if he's found some hair product to keep it perfectly in place. He's easily the most attractive person of the group and seems to have a laid-back personality. His teeth are straight, but he has a tiny gap in the front. His nose is small and narrow and his lips are tiny, but plump and pink. He has a hint of facial hair, but it's mainly stubble, giving him a slight bad boy look. His ivory skin is flaw free.

"Ignore him. He's a troublesome one. She was given the nickname long ago. Deal with it. Come here." The woman with long, wavy, strawberry blond hair and dark green eyes pulls me into a tight hug. "My name is Gwyn. The annoying one is Jayce, and the always constipated one with the scowl is Dorian." Her Irish accent tickles as she squeezes and speaks to me, her lips only inches away from my ear.

She's about 5'6", with a curvy, feminine physique. Light freckles dot her face on her high cheekbones and her narrow, pointy nose. She smiles at me with her thin lips and it's so genuine that I can't help but smile back. Gwyn is the type that back in the mortal world, people wouldn't look twice at unless she had on makeup, but I find her plain features beautiful and unique to her. Something about the hug she just gave me reminds me of my mom and I need to stop myself from tearing up.

"I am Nakayama, Kenji. Gwyn, Dorian, and I are the soul guides. It is an honor to meet you, Jasmine." Kenji bows as well looking every bit like a warrior even more so than Micah did. He's the same height as Gwyn, but has a very lean, cut body. His hair is onyx, loose and shoulder length. His brown, almond shaped eyes show pride for who he is behind them and his strong jaw gives him a serious demeanor. Yet, it's not intimidating the way Dorian's diamond shaped jaw is. Kenji isn't what I would consider to be modernly handsome, but if this was a different era, his looks would seem to be the standard.

"My name is Atara," a small voice says. I turn my head to the left where a girl with dark gray eyes and skin as caramel as mine has her hand slightly in the air. Atara has a skinny face with very delicate features. Her nose is like a button, her lips are small, but full. Her eye shape is round and innocent looking and they seem to match the shyness of the girl herself. When she turned to listen to the others, I noticed that she had an undercut, her black and teal ombre' hair shaved in the back of her head. Two intertwining hearts are cut into a design. The rest of her long hair is up in a messy bun. She looks like a model.

"I'm Cassandra. You can call me Cass or Cassie. I hate being called Sandra or Sandy. Dorian is my soul guide." Cassandra, or Cass is what I'll probably call her, has beautiful light brown eyes that I want to accentuate with eye shadow. She looks as if she had just begun filling out. Her chest is bigger than mine even though we seem to be the closest in age. Her light brunette hair is almost impossibly straight, silky, and falls to the middle of her back. Her face is oval like mine and her ridiculously straight teeth look like she was just finishing up with braces. Her thin lips are downturned in a near frown and she has an average sized pointy Roman nose. I would consider her cute or simply "plain" pretty. She's not beautiful the way I would describe Atara.

"It's nice to meet you all," I say honestly. I didn't realize how much I needed to see other people. I'm overcome with a sense of relief and longing. I really do want them to like me. "I'm Jasmine Whitmore, but I guess you all knew that. You can call me Jazzy. I'm thirteen, or was thirteen; I don't really know how that works now. Uh, I don't know what else to say."

"Is it true that you were killed by a demon?" Of course, it's Jayce that asks. He clearly doesn't have a filter. Or tact.

"Um," I hesitate.

"Come on. I know you're curious about each of our deaths. We'll share if you do." He pokes his bottom lip out again and I sigh.

"Fine. Yes. I was killed by a demon that also killed my parents. I'm still trying to come to terms with it. Not only are my mom and dad dead, but I'm here, and demons and other scary things exist and I'm supposed to help fight them. That thing that killed me was terrifying and I'm going to have to decide if I willingly fight things like that. I don't know if I can. I don't even know why I just admitted that to all of you." Tears pile up in my eyes and once again, Gwyn comes to hug me.

I even hear Jayce mutter an apology.

"This place has the ability to help us get our emotions out, especially when we don't even realize that we need to. It's a place of reflection, honesty, and peace," Micah explains. "You have every right to still feel confused and upset. I hadn't even thought about how you must feel about the thought of facing another demon. I'm sorry, again, Jasmine."

"It's okay," I manage to say, even though I don't think that it is.

"Have a seat by me, love," Gwyn offers. She walks me to her spot and rubs my back. "We've all been where you are. Given your circumstances, you were robbed of a few more precious years. None of us take that lightly. You are one of us, even if you don't feel that way. Micah may be your personal soul guide, but you can always come to any of us if you need a mentor. Even grumpy Dorian gives good advice from time to time."

Dorian snorts. "Having good insight is a trait of a strong warrior. Words solve more problems than a blade ever can."

"Thank you."

"You're welcome. Now, I'll start and then we'll go around sharing, alright. I'm Gwyn Miller and I died when I was twenty years old. My family was very poor and I lived in a time when having food in the home was a luxury. I grew up in poverty and so did my husband. We knew nothing else but our love for each other and hope that things would get better. Unfortunately, they did not. What little we did try to harvest was gone and we were on the verge of starving with an infant to feed. My husband went to go ask some neighbors for even a little bit of food. He took our son with him, hoping it would help gain sympathy. I was left alone and soon after some men broke in. They said that my husband had stolen from them and that they had tracked him here. They weren't of our town and they looked desperate. We'd had that same look in our eyes before. They were enraged when I told them that we had nothing. I couldn't return the money and they beat me to death in retaliation. Hunger and fear make you do crazy things."

I shrink back, thinking about the excessive wealth that I was used to. My father ran a billion-dollar company. I never knew what hunger was. Sitting next to Gwyn, it makes me feel ashamed, as if it's my fault that she had to go through that. It's not like I could have given her money. We come from two different worlds, two different times.

"What happened to your son?" I ask quietly.

"My husband ended up killing himself shortly after my death. He blamed himself for what happened and hopelessness had long set in for him. Our dream was never realized. I wish that he would have fought for our child. A nice couple raised my boy. He never knew about either of us. They just couldn't bear to tell him."

"I'm sorry. I don't know what else to say."

"There's nothing you can say, just listen to our stories."

"Since Gwyn is my soul guide, I'll go next. I'm Atara Adams, fifteen, and I was adopted when I was a baby. My mom had me and left me in a parking lot. No one could find my birth mom and no one stepped up to claim me. But, that's okay, because the family that did raise me was awesome. I even had a little sister. She was born about eight years after they adopted me. One day I was babysitting her while my parents were out and she wanted to play in the basement because it was cooler down there. That day was scorching outside so I couldn't blame her. I didn't know that she had taken some matches and was lighting paper and the carpet on fire until I heard the first smoke alarm."

Atara wipes her face and sighs. It takes about thirty more seconds for her to speak again. "I'm sorry. That was only a month ago. It still hurts, ya know."

"Yeah, I do. You don't have to tell me if you don't want to," I say.

"No, it's all part of the healing process. And besides, I keep my word. You shared, I share."

"Okay."

"Well, she was screaming at first, but then I heard coughing and then nothing at all. The fire spread like lightning, like I didn't even know flames could move like that. I called 911 and was crawling all over the floor searching for her. She hid and with the smoke and heat, I just couldn't find her anywhere. Then, I got lucky. I saw her hand and I dragged her to a window. I used a paint can to bust it out and screamed for help. A neighbor heard me and helped me get her to safety as I lifted her out the window. When it was my turn, I realized the window was too small for me. I tried to go back up the stairs, but... But, the ceiling collapsed and I was trapped. I got horribly burned before I even passed out from the smoke. Sometimes, I still feel like I'm on fire."

I picture firefighters pulling her burnt body from the rubble. I imagine her mom racing home while the paramedics are performing CPR in the ambulance. I think about how the doctor had to tell her family that she never made it to the hospital alive. But her sister lived. She made sure of that.

"Well, let's get this over with. I'm Dorian and I have been a soul tamer for seven hundred years. They call me The Bull. You'll soon see why when you observe me in battle. It is a name that was earned through many clashes with the enemy. I've known battle all my life. When I was alive, I was a captured after a small conflict over land and I was made a slave when I was twenty-three. They wanted to have me bow to them. I would not, so they sentenced me to death for my 'treason.' Before I could be executed, I got free and led a small slave rebellion that was unsuccessful. I was wounded badly, but alive when they captured me. They healed me, fed me, and made sure I was alive so that I could die by their hands in the manner they chose. They said that I was not going to be given the honor of dying in battle. My captors said that they wanted to mix my culture's punishment with their own. I was stripped naked, stoned nearly to death, dragged by horse and then thrown from a cliff."

"That's horrible!" I can't help but to voice. He went through it. I don't need to tell him that.

"Others have gone through worse. Those times were cruel to us all. I've long moved on, young one. I will never forget what was done to me, but in order to keep going, you cannot carry all of your pain with you."

I give him a soft smile, but my heart isn't into it. He's had seven hundred years to move on. It's only been a matter of days for me. Ask me again in one hundred years.

The brunette goes next. "I'm Cassandra St. John. Fourteen years old. My mom was an Italian immigrant and met my dad when he was on a business trip. They fell in love and she moved to America to be with him. I grew up on the East Coast and traveled a lot because of my dad's job. We had only been in town for about five months and I wanted to still do some exploring one weekend. I got turned around and my phone lost service. I asked this guy for help, but he knocked me out and took me. He was a serial killer. I don't want to talk about the details. That was about three months ago." Cassandra puts her hair behind her ear and turns away.

Kenji's voice claims the silence. "I was sixteen when my trial came. My family wasn't rich, but we weren't poor either. We lived in a modern village for the time and were under strict rule. There were five of us in my family- all boys except for my youngest sister. One of my brothers had already left our home and started a family, so I was the next eldest. My younger brother was a troublemaker and it was often my responsibility to clean up his mess. He stole from a nobleman and fled, but was caught. One of the man's horses got injured in the chase. He demanded a heavy payment for that. Not only did my brother dishonor us, he crossed a very dangerous man. He wanted me to kill my brother in retribution. My parents were too afraid to do anything to make the situation worse, but I refused and told him that I would take my own life instead. Before anyone could stop me, I ran the sword through my stomach."

"You saved your brother. You're a hero."

"I was his protector, always. I will never regret my sacrifice. I would do it one thousand times to save him Now, who do we have left?"

"Saved the best for last, of course." Jayce smiles. Only he would smile before he tells a more than likely morbid story of his demise. Something tells me that he smiles a lot.

"I'm Jayce Harper. I'm seventeen and was raised in the U.S. Three years ago, I moved to France with my parents. They had some government jobs or something. Anyway, I met this guy and we started dating for about a year. Some idiots didn't like that we were together. The final straw was us holding hands and minding our own business, apparently. They followed us back to his place. We were all drunk and I wasn't paying attention to my surroundings, didn't think I needed to. They beat us both severely, but I fought back and took most of the hits. I was in a coma for a couple of days, but there was too much brain damage. My parents had to pull the plug on me."

"They did that to you just because you like boys. I hate the world sometimes. People are just so, so..." I struggle to find the word.

"People are afraid of what they don't understand," Jayce says. "So I like boys and girls. I like to think of myself as open to all possibilities in love. That makes me special, not disgusting."

I see Jayce in a different light. He's not as shallow as his demeanor led me to believe. There's an intelligence and deep hurt behind those shining, bright eyes. It makes me want to hold him, to protect him from something that's already been done. "You're no different from anyone else. There's nothing wrong with loving someone of the same sex." I think of my sister. I couldn't bear the thought of someone trying to do her harm because she's with Selene.

"Thank you. I keep trying to tell Dorian that, but he's not hearing it," Jayce says with a smirk.

"It's just not going to happen. I can't change that I am not attracted to men any more than you can change that you're attracted to, well, everyone in the world," Dorian shoots back.

"Aww, you're no fun, and you're stereotyping. I'm not just some horny bisexual boy that will hump anything. I have standards, okay."

"Yes, and I have very particular standards. Don't make me kick your ass."

Jayce laughs and his eyes shine, but behind them, I see something else. Regret. He misses his boyfriend. He's an expert at hiding his emotions behind that heart-stopping smile, but I already know what to look for. Atara glances at me and then him. She sees it too. I look at everyone here, how they easily opened up to me and told me the truth of their suffering. It makes me want to protect them all somehow. I want to be a part of their world, their ally, their friend. We are all bonded by our pain.

I speak up, cutting through the voices of chatter as everyone splits up into smaller conversations. I look Micah in the eye and smile. "I'd like to hear more about what we do, if that's okay."

Chapter Six

*W*hen I fall asleep, I have nightmares about every single one of their stories. I'm put into their bodies and I share their final moments. I wake up wide eyed, a particular feeling in the pit of my stomach. Fear. 'I'm safe here,' I remind myself. Those were just dreams. All of that never happened to me.

But it did happen.

Horrible things happen like that every day.

Kenji said that if dark spirits were to possess human bodies, even more horrible things would happen. Demons that consume multiple souls can gain tremendous strength. Souls that are consumed in this world don't pass on. They are never reborn. We keep that from happening.

I force myself to get up and shake off my hesitation. I've decided to move forward. I will do my best to stick with it.

Today is meditation day. Micah and I are going to get me to merge my energy with his so that I can sense him the way he senses me. Once that's completed, we'll be training with the others. But, it might take days, depending on my spirit energy. Some people are more connected than others. It may not be my strong suit.

We go back to the large meditation grounds where I met the group and place ourselves on a set of pillows near a section of perfectly combed sand. I get fascinated all over again with the way the open structure seems to have grown right out of the earth as the vines and trees fuse with it as if they made the area themselves. The oper ceiling gives a perfect view of the multicolored blue sky.

I wonder if the candles ever burn out or if they just belong to the world as well. The rocks that are laid out in patterns are different sizes and colors and remind me of rocks that you'd find in the desert or a canyon. They surround the tiny ponds of crystal water and I refrain from reaching in and trying to see if I can taste the water because it looks so refreshing.

We walk up a set of three steps and stop next to a group of royal purple pillows that remind me of large dog beds. Micah faces me with a serious expression. He's dressed how he was when we first met. His pants barely touch his ankles and he's wearing no shoes. The bright, but comfortable sun shines off his defined muscles.

"Take my hand Jasmine."

I put my small hands in his, noticing the warmth and familiarity of them He closes his large hands over mine firmly. They are rough and masculine. I like touching his hand. It makes me feel safe.

"Now, depending on your level of comfort, this may seem intimate. But, I will not let you feel uncomfortable. If you must pull away, do so. You won't hurt my feelings and we'll just have to start over."

"Okay. I think I'll be fine though."

"Good. Whenever you're ready to get started, just take a deep breath and close your eyes."

I nod. A few seconds later, I inhale slowly, releasing it as I close my eyes. Micah's grip tightens around mine and for about a minute, he says nothing. A minute turns into two, and then I open one eye.

"You're supposed to be focused," he chastises.

"On what though? We're not doing anything."

"We are. You're learning how to be still and just relax. I can't do anything else until then. Focus on the serenity around you. Listen to the sound of the world, the quiet, the sense of comfort it gives you. Just unwind."

"Okay, I'll try." I close my eyes again and take a deep breath.

I last five minutes this time before I sigh deeply. Touching Micah this long has started to get uncomfortable. I slowly pull my hands away and rub them as if I've gotten a cramp. He doesn't say anything about it. He just waits quietly for me to put my hands in his again.

"This isn't working."

"We haven't been at it for long."

"No, I know when things are working for me, even if I don't catch on. This isn't going to work. I need you to give me something specific to focus on. Just telling me to think about the world around me is too much. It's actually making it harder for me."

"Okay, well, what makes you feel joy? What do you like to do that requires you to concentrate for long periods at a time without you even noticing?"

"Painting," I say immediately.

"Good." He reaches for my hands again. "Tell me about the process."

"Well, I usually get my inspiration from the world around me. I'll see something pretty and I'll be like ooh, I want to paint that. I like scenery or things in the background that people don't really pay attention to."

Micah stares deeply into my eyes, hanging onto every word. He rubs the back of my hands and I begin to relax.

"Then, I have to prep by getting all of my supplies together. I like to work with acrylic or oil pastels, but I'll use watercolors or oil paint too. I've done some airbrushing in the past, but it's not what I'm an expert at. That is fun for making clothes though. But, anyway, I get all my supplies, my pencils, my sketchbook, my canvas set up, my paints, and I go work on my sketch first. I usually return to where I found my inspiration, or I'll go online and see if I can find something similar. Sometimes, I'll do it from memory or I'll remember to take a picture beforehand."

"Sounds like a process."

"It is. But, I love it. I like to sketch with music. I listen to old school stuff like Lauryn Hill, Run-D.M.C., Michael Jackson, Elton John, Earth Wind & Fire, Jimi Hendrix, all that. It just depends on my mood and what I'm painting. Then, I get to work."

"What does painting feel like?"

"For me, freedom. I'm not just in my house anymore, I'm everywhere, I feel connected to everything. Every stroke of my brush or swipe of my wrist gives me the power to make something beautiful.

I'm a perfectionist when it comes to that. I can spend hours working on a few lines making sure they are exactly how I need them to be. It's my own creation and I don't do it for anyone else but me. That's what makes me happy. I'm in control of it and I'm free to make what I choose."

"It sounds beautiful. You create these moments in time forever frozen by your vision. Eternal flower, indeed."

I tilt my head and look at Micah. "I don't want to just be this pretty girl that's tragically stuck as a thirteen-year-old for eternity. That's not how I want everyone to see me."

"They won't. You will prove that your beauty is far beyond the flesh you wear. You make everything about your existence striking. You're not just a pretty face. I don't think that."

"Okay. Because that's what people always think about me. Sometimes, I don't think I'm taken seriously."

"We don't think that. You're here for a purpose, remember? We see you for who you are."

"It's just that when Dorian called me that, it made me uncomfortable as if he was being condescending."

"That's just how he comes off. Do you not like it?"

"No, I kinda do. Besides, Jayce said the others don't have nicknames. It's cool that I do, even if I haven't exactly earned it."

"But you have. We've been calling you that for years."

"Oh."

"Sorry. I just reminded you that your death was planned, again, didn't I?"

I ignore his question. "So, what's the rest of your nicknames?"

He plays along. "Well, Dorian already said that he's The Bull. Kenji is called Shadow Walker because he can track souls into the darkest realms, even when the soul's resonance is incredibly faint. Gwyn is called the Blood Fox. She's a wonderful person, but she enjoys the hunt and the kill much more than the rest of us. She likes when it gets... messy. But, she's smart. Out of every one of us, even more so than Dorian, she was built for this, believe it or not."

"And what do they call you, Micah?"

"I am The Silver Phoenix. You've seen the flames of my blade, but my flames turn silver when I'm using the limit of my power. I'm able to create an inferno that when I focus, resembles a phoenix. So, it's only fitting."

"Does it come out of your sword?"

"It can, but our power comes within. We each have a weapon. Well, usually only one. Some can claim more. Along with that, some of us can manipulate one element. All of this is chosen for us. We are given the things that best suit us and our skills."

"Ugh, so complicated."

He laughs. "It sounds like it, but it's really not. I was given a katana. My element is fire and it works for me. For instance, Gwyn uses a hammer, her element is earth."

"Yeah, my head hurts."

"Let's stop for today. But, tomorrow, we're going to focus." He gives me a look that teachers give bad students.

"Fine, but how about you teach me to change my clothes first and then I could probably get the hang of us connecting."

"No. That will be your incentive. Master our connection first. Looking nice will come later."

"Fine. You're no fun. Don't forget, you technically are still a teenager. Loosen up."

He snorts. "Somehow, I feel like I'll have to be more like a parent with you."

"I plead the fifth."

"You're free for now, Miss Whitmore. I will see you later." He stands up and wipes himself off as he walks away and vanishes mid-stride.

"Show off."

"Good, he's gone. Now the party can start. Hey, Jazzy."

I look around to see where my new visitor came from. He was probably hiding behind a wall, waiting to annoy me.

"Hello Jayce. Aren't you supposed to be training or something?"

"Nah. We finished up a little bit ago. I wanted to know if you wanted to go for a walk and swim with me?"

"Sure, I'll go swim with you, just let me go get my swimsuit. I'll just go pull it out my suitcase." I raise my eyebrow at him.

"Oh, so you haven't learned that little trick yet?"

"Nope. He won't teach me until we gain our connection."

"That's lame."

"My thoughts exactly. So, I can go with you, but I don't want to walk around in wet clothes after. And why don't they have wardrobe choices for those of us that haven't grasped the skill of instant wardrobe changes?"

"Well, it's not like we need to really change clothes, unless we get blood or guts on them. We don't need to shower or use the bathroom and if we sweat, we don't stink. We don't eat, so we're not going to drop food on ourselves. Don't you think it's pretty incredible how we still keep some of our human traits? Like, we're not ghosts or spirits. We're real. In this world at least we can touch, we can still feel. It's not so bad. Take advantage of it, unless you just want to wait for your boss." His expression is defiant. He's testing me.

"Okay, I get it." I roll my eyes and pout. "I still want to learn it. I love clothes."

"Hey, so do I." Jayce gets up and his clothes shimmer until he's now wearing a blue fitted V-neck that matches his eyes and black jeans that fit tightly. Then, he changes until he's in yellow swim trunks with silver stars. Show off.

"Those are ugly," I lie, with a smile.

"Good thing you're not wearing them, then. Hey, why don't I just teach you? If that doesn't work, I can just conjure up some shorts and a t-shirt for you and give them to you."

"Okay. We can try. Micah's going to be mad."

"No, he'll be impressed that you worked so hard on your own."

"Hmm, I like that better."

"I'm very persuasive." He winks. "Okay. Let's see. It's simple, much easier than the connection thingy. You have to imagine the clothes. Think of the color, the feel of the fabric against your skin, its warmth. Visualize the details clearly and then imagine it covering you, your body in all the places that it's supposed to. Can you do that?"

"We'll see, won't we? I close my eyes and take my time picturing my favorite two-piece swimsuit. It's turquoise with a triple crossing back strap and has a short skirt look for the bottom. I imagine the spandex material pressing against my body and the contrast of my exposed skin and my covered limbs. I try to picture every detail that I remember about it and how pretty I feel in it.

After a few seconds, Jayce says, "Okay, that's kind of cute. I love the color."

I grin and peek one eye open. "I did it?"

He nods.

I jump up and pat my body, looking at the two-piece adorning my skin. "Dope!"

"Dope indeed.' He laughs, shakes his head and then holds out an arm for me to slide my arm in between. Then, he escorts me out of the meditation area as I giggle in delight, glad to have mastered something so quickly.

I can't wait to go back home and practice, but for now, I'll be content to hang out with Jayce. We fall into a comfortable silence as we make our way through the beautiful landscape around us.

Finally, I speak up. "My sister's a lesbian and I know how hard it can be if you don't have someone to talk about things like that that are bothering you. So, if you ever want to vent or talk about your boyfriend, I'm here to listen or whatever. I won't think it's weird or gross, or wrong, okay."

Jayce stiffens, but continues to walk without saying a word. Instead, he squeezes my shoulder and I smile. No other words are said until we reach the black sand of "Afterlife Lake," as I've decided to name it. Then, Jayce wastes no time running and diving in I quickly follow.

It's eerie The water is so crystal clear that I can see to the bottom, but there are no fish or other aquatic animals to been seen. Other than a few underwater plants, the lake is nothing more than a beautiful pool. We race, splash each other, and then are content to float on our backs.

"This is nice," I admit. The water isn't cold at all. It's almost as if all my stress is washing away with the water. I feel stronger, more of myself than I have since I've been here. "You're a sneaky thing, you know that."

"Whatever do you mean?" he asks as if he's confused.

"Thank you, Jayce."

"You're welcome, Jasmine Whitmore."

He knew what the water would do to me, how I needed to relax and feel renewed. How I needed to do something normal.

"So, what's it been like since you got here?"

"Well, it's been a lot of chilling, meditation, a tiny bit of training, and... waiting, for you."

"Why?"

"Because even though most tamers fight alone, they're trying something new with us. We're going to be a type of special ops team with a specific expertise. They haven't told us what that is yet. Looks like they already think that we're badass."

"Well, it's probably true," I add with a smile. It's frightening to think about though. We may be dead, but we're still just kids.

"We should come up with a team name. I mean, you have the *Teen Titans, Avengers, Justice League,* and others. But, we're really superheroes. I'll sleep on it. The Shadow Spirits. No, the Spirit Kings. Is that sexist? How about-,"

"Jayce."

"Hmm."

"Sleep on it."

He laughs. "Those were good names."

I splash him and he yells in protest. "Eternal flower? How about eternal asshole," he mutters.

"Aww, are you worried about your hair, Casanova?"

"Please. My hair stays perfect in all elements."

I shake my head. This is probably what having a brother feels like. Jayce and I float our cares away until the sun starts to go down. A couple people had passed by during our time in the water, but none have bothered us. I'm not used to this type of quiet. I love the city life, the constant buzz of life. Like being dead, this will take some getting used to.

Chapter Seven

*B*y the time I get to my room and changed, I'm much more tired than I'd realized. I plop down on my impossibly soft bed and am out like a light. I never even made it under the covers. When I awaken, Micah's sitting on my bed, staring out the window.

"Creepy much," I say, voice thick with sleep after I get over my initial startle. My eyes still take a minute to adjust.

He's wearing dark green sweat pants and a white t-shirt. His hair is once again braided, but there are a few fly-aways as if he's been working out. His arms are crossed and the sleeves of his shirt ride up with the flex of his muscles.

"You learned how to change your clothes, I see." He looks at me and frowns at my little black shorts and gray t-shirt.

"Are you mad?" I ask, fluttering my eyelashes.

"Maybe a little. I gave you an order and you had someone teach you about fashion instead. You picked it up fast and that's impressive, but still. I need to know I can trust you to do as I ask."

"It wasn't like that." I run my fingers through my hair and sit up straighter. "Jayce wanted to go swimming and I didn't have the clothes. It was necessary."

"Yes, swimming was so necessary."

"The way the water helped me feel was necessary.

He stiffens at my comment. "I- I wanted to talk to you about your sister."

I'm completely awake now. "What's wrong? What happened?"

"Well, it's been a little over a week since you've passed and they've buried your family. Of course, she couldn't go because they're saying she was killed too, to protect her, but-,"

"What?"

"She's not really fully conscious or should I say coherent. She's been given sedatives, but every time she wakes up, they've had to wrestle with her and sedate her again. She's not taking your deaths well and she's fighting her recovery. Her body is still in fight or flight mode. I just thought that you should know."

"Well, tell someone to do something to help her and I'll do whatever you want. Just fix her."

"We can't."

"The hell you can't. Someone can."

"We just have to see how this plays out. If she's anything like you, she'll get through it."

"She's better than me."

"I don't believe that."

"I mean she always finds a way to win. I'm usually the one to give up."

"Well, don't give up on Rayne. She'll pull through. Selene had a healer try to mend her shattered ankle and it just may have been too much. I don't know. It was a heck of a fight from what I understand. She was choked, thrown around, had her ankle completely shattered, and saw the aftermath of what was done to you. Selene used her magic to hold the demon at bay. I think it was her first time in an encounter like that as well. She has Selene to lean on. She will bring her back and help her heal."

"I'll try not to worry, but please keep me informed."

"I will. I promise."

"Why else are you here, Micah?"

"We need to get our connection underway. Everyone is ready to start training with us."

I yawn. "Fine. Let's do this." I slide to the floor and pull Micah with me. "Eyes closed, mind clear, breathe slowly, what else?"

"Why are you in such a rush to learn this now?"

"I had fun hanging out with Jayce. I want to see him and the others again."

"Do you like him? Like a crush?"

I laugh, "Who, Casanova? Nah. He's cute and all, but he's a little too cocky and old for me. But, I like him as a friend. He's cool."

"Oh, okay."

"Why, do you like him?"

"Huh? No, I don't like boys."

"Just checking."

"Can we change the subject, please." Micah rubs the back of his head and blushes. He clearly likes someone. I'll find out who later.

"Okay, let's try again."

He grabs my hands. We close our eyes. "Focus on me. Match your breathing to mine. Picture me in your head and then picture something that makes you feel safe. Associate the two together and picture us connected by an invisible thread that only you can see."

I do as I'm told, first clearing my mind and taking cleansing breaths. It takes me over ten minutes to clear my mind enough to even begin to do the things he said. Finally, I relax enough and match my slow breathing to Micah's even slower breaths. It takes me even longer to think about something that makes me feel safe and to associate it with him.

I try twice, my frustration making it hard to focus. Micah encourages me to start over and after three tries, I begin to feel a hint of a pull between the two of us. I imagine my hands reaching for and grabbing that thread. Once I touch it in my mind, it becomes brighter.

Can you hear me? Micah asks in my head.

Yeah, I say trying to keep my eyes shut. *This is pretty cool.*

It is. Now, I'm going to leave and you need to find me. I won't go far so it shouldn't be too hard. Once you locate me, travel there by locking onto my energy.

Okay.

Think you can do that?

Yeah, I can.

He smiles, lets my hands go, and disappears. I stand up, take my time changing into a pair of designer sunglasses, a black pair of skinny jeans, a red cardigan, and red gladiator shoes with a small heel. Then, I take a deep breath and feel for Micah's energy. It takes me only thirty seconds to find him. I picture him as clearly as I can in my head and me next to him.

It happens almost instantly. Micah turns to me with half a smile on his face and then it fades when he sees my outfit change.

"Really?" He rolls his eyes.

"What? I just wanted to show you how good at this I am."

"I had to get partnered with the fashionista."

"Aw, don't complain, you might hurt my feelings." I pout and Micah turns red.

"I-I'm sorry."

I can't help but laugh. "Relax. I was just joking. It takes more than that to hurt my feelings."

"Well, girls are complicated. There's no telling how you really feel. You may say that you're fine, but inside your head, you're thinking of multiple ways to hurt me."

Now, I really laugh. "You are funny."

"What did I say?"

I shake my head. "Nothing. What's next?"

"Well, now we meet with the others. They should be arriving soon. Follow me." Micah disappears again and I attempt to follow his soul's resonance to find him. Again, it takes about thirty seconds to find and reach my soul guide.

"Good job," he says once I appear.

I look at my surroundings. We seem to be in another part of the world. It's grassy and windy, making the grass seem like an ocean wave of green. Dorian and Cass appear next. Dorian scans the landscape as I did, no doubt searching for something particular. His gaze lands on me and he nods. I nod back and wave at Cass.

"Hey," she responds, just as Atara, Gwyn, Jayce, and Kenji all appear in quick succession.

Jayce puts an arm around Kenji's shoulder and whispers something. Kenji snorts and pushes him away playfully. Atara gives me a warm smile and then slips behind Gwyn who hugs everyone within range. After all greetings are exchanged, Dorian steps to the center.

"Finally, we're all here and ready to begin. Each day, first thing, us guides will come get you and we will train together as a group. Then, you will spend some time working one on one with your guide. After that you will mediate or go on missions with your guide if they choose to allow it. Every once in a while, we will go and pick one of you to train with, to help with what your guide is teaching you." He looks around waiting for us to ask questions. We don't.

"Now, I suggest that you change into something more comfortable and easier to move in," Kenji says.

We all sigh and take our time changing into tank tops, shorts, t-shirts, sweats, and yogas. I'm wearing my favorite gray and pink yoga pants from Victoria's Secret and a light pink tank top. Dorian is shirtless, Kenji is wearing a black sleeveless gi and pants, Gwyn has on tight green yoga Capri pants that fit snugly on around her calf and a white half-shirt, and Micah is also shirtless. The rest of them look like we're going to the gym.

Gwyn steps forward with a smile and the rest of the guides take about three steps back. "I'm up first. We're going to play a game of tag."

"Huh?" Cass asks.

"You heard me, didn't ya? Tag, girly."

"Okay, tag."

"Would ya let me explain the rules or are you goin' to just look at me like I'm crazy?" Her Irish accent is thick with impatience.

"Sorry."

"Good, now, the point of this lil game is to get you to work on your travel speed. We chose this place for this exercise because it's wide open and there's nowhere to get lost, unless you're really thick in the head. One of you will be 'it' and the rest of ya have to move around with your power to get away. It's simple."

Simple she says. Somehow, I doubt that.

"I'll be goin' first. I'll count ta ten and I suggest you run. One, two. I've always been a bit impatient-ten!" Gwyn steps forward and we either squeal or try to disappear.

It's hard under pressure and I swear I can feel my heart beating in my chest as I try to melt in and out of existence. It doesn't happen the way I planned and soon, Gwyn is looking in my direction. I turn to run away, but she pops up in front of me and I fall backwards. She touches my shoulder and disappears.

I frown and look up at the other three guides that are crowded around each other laughing and whispering. Micah motions for me to stand and then points to the others that are having just a bit of difficulty too. Jayce has his back to me and he keeps nodding his head like a genie as if that's going to help him get the hang of it quicker. I sneak over to him but just as I get ready to touch him, he disappears.

"This is stupid!"

"Only if you suck." Jayce's voice comes from behind me.

I turn around and glare at him and he disappears again about fifty feet from me.

"Concentrate," Micah says.

"I'm trying."

"You know how to do it. You're not jumping worlds, you're just moving faster in this one. Think about it."

"Ugh."

They all laugh again and I glare once more, attempting to pop up in front of them. Dorian notices first and disappears leaving Micah and Kenji laughing together. I touch Kenji on the side of his arm and run.

"I wasn't in the game," he calls after me.

"You are now," Gwyn says to him.

"Fine." He huffs and then wastes no time tagging Cass who yelps as he swiftly appears in front of her and then he proceeds to show off by popping up in quick succession next to all of us.

Cassandra is pretty good and tries to go after Jayce, but he's on to her and jumps behind me. I spin away from him at the last second and she ends up tagging him anyway. It gives me enough time to get away. He goes after Atara and she manages to dodge him for a little while before she grows tired. She ends up giving up and lets him tag her hand.

"Boooo!" Micah calls. He turns both thumbs down. "You can't just give up like that."

Atara sits down in a huff and Micah frowns, walking over to her, not even realizing that he's falling for the oldest trick in the book. When he gets within range, she touches him and then disappears. Dorian lets out a bellowing laugh and Micah proceeds to chase him. They look like lightening bugs the way their energy pops up all over the place lighting up the world.

Finally, Micah gives up and goes after an easier target, me.

But, I'm ready and since I can feel his energy, I am able to dodge most of his attempts. He smiles approvingly at me and then moves on to tag Atara once again as payback. We all continue this game for a while, each of us getting faster, even just by a bit. By the time it's over, we're all extremely worn out. We sit in a circle and catch our breath for a few minutes.

"Pair up," Dorian orders.

"Jazzy," Jayce declares quickly. Atara gives him a look, but I can't figure out why.

"Okay," I say and move to sit by him.

"We're going to work on some fighting techniques. Do any of you have experience already?"

Cassandra raises her hand and so do I. I don't have much, that's for sure, but my dad was teaching Rayne and sometimes I came in and tried too. Cassandra looks at me and gives me a skeptical look. Great, she already thinks I'm some kind of prissy queen.

"Well, it doesn't matter what your experience level was or is, we will make you into masters. Fighting dark spirits and demons will not be like fighting humans. There are other techniques that we will show you, but hand to hand combat can also help because you may encounter souls that have escaped from a hell dimension."

Yeah, that doesn't sound scary at all. Nope.

"So, stand up, face your partner, and I will walk you through the first step. We are beings of energy and of flesh. We must be able to feel and understand the way we did as mortals, but we are also beyond that. We can sense life force and movements. That is what helps us fight and anticipate our opponents. You may have a bond with your soul guide, but all of our energy is available for you to feel."

Dorian closes his eyes and extends his arms. "No one alive will ever be as connected as we are now. Take advantage of it."

I close my eyes too and breathe. I try to feel the energy of those around me like tiny flames. I know that they're there, but it's hard to feel them all at once. I open my eyes again to find Jayce watching me in amusement. I roll my eyes.

"Once you feel your partner's energy, I want one of you to close your eyes and mimic the other's movements. Keep doing it until you get it right and then switch."

The others circle around us, watching and ready to correct any mistakes that we make. Jayce closes his eyes first and I lift my left arm. I hold it there for about twenty seconds before he lifts his right arm, a mirror reflection of my own. Then, I lower it until I'm touching the top of my head. He does the same thing. I try a few other motions, a little more complicated, confident that he can do those as well. Then, we switch.

"Hey, we could do some awesome choreography like this," I joke.

He laughs as he spins around in a circle. I do the same. Clearing of a throat brings us back to what we're doing. But, we look at each other and smile. He bows dramatically and winks at Dorian who shakes his head and crosses his arms.

"He's going to rip your arms off," I warn. "Leave that man alone."

"Oh, I know I have no chance. I just like to get under his skin. He's so uptight."

"Well, be careful. I don't want you really catching feelings for him and getting hurt."

"I'll be fine, Jazzy. Besides, I'm having too much fun playing match maker right now." He tilts his head over to Cass and Atara who is having just a little bit of issue with staring at Cassandra's face while her eyes are closed.

"Seriously. They like each other?"

"Uh, I don't know about crabby pants, I mean Cassandra, but Atara likes her, she just doesn't realize it yet. I don't think she knows what she likes."

"Hmm, well don't try to push them into something that they're not ready for."

"I'm not. I'm just helping move things along either way."

"And what if it doesn't work out?"

"Then, at least she'll know and can move on."

"Fair enough, I guess."

Dorian speaks up again, grabbing our attention. "Now, I'm going to show you some cycles to run through. These will be offensive and then we'll move into defensive. Watch closely."

Dorian's muscles ripple as he drops low into a firm stance and begins the first set. I look around and everyone's eyes are on him. Nope, no problem with people watching him closely.

Well, I am here to learn. I better pay close, close attention.

"The first step is to make sure you have good balance. Every movement that you make will not be wasted. You will move like living art when I'm through with you."

I do enjoy a good piece of art.

Chapter Eight

I beg Micah for the seventh time to stop for today. "I'm exhausted. Pleeeeease."

He mocks me, "Noooooo. You're not done, lazy pants. Now, block."

I hold up my hands and block his slow punches. When he sees me slowly lowering my hands, he punches faster, startling me. "Hey!"

"It's not like it'll kill you. Pay attention."

"You're an a-hole."

"Me, nah. I'm the nice one. Keep blocking." He starts to kick and alternate between punches. "Feel my energy. I'm about to move faster."

Despite my fatigue, I do as I'm told and can keep up with most of his movements. Slowly though, I'm worn down even more and a punch connects with my shoulder. It hurts but I wave Micah away when he tries to comfort me. I can take one little punch.

"I'm just worn out from the energy thing."

"Okay, fine. Go meditate and then get some rest. I'll come to you in the morning. We're going to train even longer tomorrow."

I sigh. "Fine. I'll see you tomorrow."

"Bye, Jasmine."

"Wait," I call before he disappears. His long, braided ponytail sways side to side as he turns. "What do you do in your free time? What can I do in mine?"

"Well, I'm usually on patrol. I train a lot with Gwyn and I spend time traveling to places that I never got to see when I was alive."

"Maybe you can take me with you one day."

"Maybe. Have a good night, Jasmine."

"You too, Micah."

Once he leaves, I take my time walking to the meditation area and sit next to the Shishi odoshi, a Japanese bamboo fountain that tilts and pours out water once it's too heavy. The rhythmic tapping relaxes me. I sit, close my eyes, and think about my family, ignoring the fact that he never answered my question.

◊◊◊

I knock two times on the door and then push it open a crack, waking my parents up. "Mommy, daddy, can I lay with you tonight?" I ask quietly, clutching my green stuffed dinosaur with yellow spots and big eyes. "Rayne said that my room was haunted by ghosts of kids that the Boogeyman got." Tears fill my eyes as I remember the story my big sister told me after I got into her make-up collection.

"I'm going to have a talk with that girl in the morning," my daddy says before scooting over. I shuffle in my jammies to the bed and he lifts me up. Then, he reaches over and grabs his white tank top from the floor and puts it on.

My mom rolls over and runs a finger through my long hair, brushing it out my eyes. Her own long hair is wild and sticking up at different angles. She then places a kiss on my forehead. "There is no such thing as the Boogeyman, sweetheart. Even if there was, there's no way your daddy would let him anywhere near you."

I gulp and nod My dad rubs my back. "What about ghosts?"

"You don't have to worry about them either, Jazzy Jazz. We'll protect you always."

I wrap my little arms around my mom's neck and kiss her loudly on her cheek. "Okay," I whisper. "Night, night."

My daddy chuckles. "Night, night, baby girl."

Another memory reveals itself.

"What's wrong, Jasmine? Why are you running away?" my big sister asks me as I stuff my favorite book bag full of clothes. She came to see if I wanted to take a swim with her, but caught me packing instead.

She's wearing a flowy wine colored dress. Her dark wavy hair falls down her back and she has a pair of sunglasses on the top of her head. Her inquiring hazel eyes are like mirrors of my own. Her full lips are pursed as she watches me. One of her perfect eyebrows is raised.

"I don't want to talk about it," I say biting my lower lip to keep from crying. She always called me a crybaby when I didn't get my way. I'm determined to prove her wrong.

She sighs and closes the door to my bedroom. I look around and think about taking my dinosaur or a Barbie. I'm going to miss the bright rainbow colors in my room and my big bed with my princess covers.

"You're nine years old. You can't just run away. Tell me what's going on and then we can fix it," she says.

I stop what I'm doing. "Promise you won't tell?"

"Pinky swear."

"I don't want to go to school anymore."

"Why? You love school."

"Be-because two boys said that I'm stupid and ripped up my spelling test. Then, one pushed me and called me ugly." Tears flow freely now.

"Did you tell the teacher? Did an adult see it happen?"

"No. We were getting ready to go to lunch. They said if I come back tomorrow, they were going to beat me up."

"Okay, first," Rayne pulls me in for a tight hug. "You are most definitely *not* ugly. You are very beautiful, Jazzy. Second, you're a Whitmore. There's no way possible that you could be stupid." She pulls away from me and wipes my eyes. "What did you get on your spelling test?"

"A ninety-five. I had to rewrite the words I missed five times."

"Good job. I bet you won't miss them again."

I shake my head, agreeing that I won't.

"And what did those boys get?"

I shrug.

"Exactly. That's because they did worse than you and were jealous You're awesome. Jazzy, some people must be mean to others to make themselves feel better. You're not like that. They probably like you too and don't know how to show it. Little boys are like that. It's not right, but they often bully girls that they like because they weren't taught manners."

"Did you ever get bullied by boys?" I sniffle.

"A little bit. But, I usually beat them up and they left me alone." Rayne laughs and winks at me.

"I don't like to hit though."

"You don't have to. But, me and you need to tell your teacher tomorrow because if you don't tell them to stop now, then they'll think they have permission to treat you bad."

"You'll come with me?"

"Of course. We'll ride to school together. I can be a little late. Just don't tell mom, okay." She ruffles my hair.

"Okay. Rayne, did you ever like the boys that bullied you?"

Rayne looks at me for a few seconds as if she doesn't know how to answer. "Uh, I didn't really like the boys at all."

"What about now? Do you have a boy you like?"

She sighs and sits on the floor, crossing her legs. After a minute of frowning and staring at me, she says, "Jasmine, I don't like boys. I like girls." She hangs her head down and I can't understand why my strong, confident sister looks so ashamed.

"Oh. Well, what kind of girls do you like?"

She looks up at me in surprise. "Um, well, I guess I like girls that look like princesses."

My eyes light up. "Ooh, like princess Jasmine?"

She laughs. "Yeah, something like that. But, don't tell mom I told you, okay. It's our secret."

"Why?"

"Um, because I don't want mom or dad to be mad at me if they find out before I tell them.

I wrap my arms around her waist. "Okay. I love you, Rayne."

She hugs me back. "I love you too, Jazzy poo."

◊◊◊

I open my eyes and start to cry as I think about those couple of times with my family. I was able to make so many wonderful memories in my short life that I feel like I can't even complain. Most people never experienced half of what I could because of the opportunities my family's wealth afforded me or the fact that my family was tight-knit. But, it still hurts like hell and I can't even pretend that I'm yet okay with us being separated forever.

I just want one more hug, one more kiss, one more car ride, one last trip.

I sob into my hands and pray that my parents are in a better place and that my sister fights through her own demons. Then, I pray that I find the strength to keep going, the same way Micah, Gwyn, Kenji, and Dorian have. To find the splendor in the tragedy that was my circumstance.

Finally, the tears pause and I feel just a bit lighter. After I finish meditating, I'll go for a quick swim alone to relax and then maybe I'll get to know the others better. After all, it seems that I'm going to be with them for a very long time.

Chapter Nine

We all sit in Atara's room and laugh as she tells us about the time she poured a whole lot of salt instead of sugar in her mom's coffee. Once we finish wiping the tears from our eyes, we all settle into a comfortable silence. I take the time to look around the room. Her room is the same layout as mine, probably the same as all of ours, but that's where the similarities end.

Her room is a mix of many shades of blue. She has a hardwood floor instead of carpet and thick blue rugs with swirls. There's a spinning chair hanging from the ceiling and a vanity over in one corner. She even has a desk with books sitting atop it and a window sill that extends where she can sit and look out of it if she chooses. Her large, circular bed sits in the middle of the floor and is covered with stuffed animals. She even has a unique circular set of lighting that hangs from the ceiling. We're all sitting in beanbag chairs.

"So, if you were still alive, what would you be doing right now?" Atara asks. She looks at Cass first who pulls her pillow in closer to her body.

"Well, I'd probably be outside playing sports. Skateboarding, running track, soccer, whatever. I never had a favorite sport, so I tried to be good at as many as I could. I'd be hanging out with my friends and planning a cross-country trip that my mom would never let me take." Cass stares off into the distance as she thinks about it. If she's like me, it's something that she's been thinking about every day.

"My parents were great, but they were so busy all the time that I learned to do a lot of things without them. It's okay though, because they taught me to rely on myself and I appreciate that. But, when we did have time to hang out together, my mom would always try to make this big family dinner that she'd burn and so my dad who was the real cook would whip something else up or we'd order take out. But, sometimes, me and my dad would just suck it up and eat it anyway just because she tried." Cass laughs and it's full of sorrow that sets my own heart aching. "My mom was good at a lot of things. Cooking was like her arch nemesis. If I was back there right now, my dad and I would probably be eating burnt macaroni and arm wrestling."

Her voice trails off and she has that faraway gaze once again. If she had the ability to see what they were doing right now, she'd look in on them in a heartbeat. She's worried about how they're going to deal with an empty chair for dinner every night. Something tells me that they'll both bury themselves in work. I hope that they can find a way to get through this.

"I'd be outside taking pictures with the photography class I signed up for. Then, I'd be trying to convince my friends to go to a museum or something with me. They'd say no and we'd probably go swimming instead." Atara smiles softly. "They never really liked doing the stuff that I liked to do. I don't really have this big story to tell about a great adventure. I babysat a lot and hung out every occasionally. That's pretty much it." She shrugs.

"Why did you get into photography?" I ask to keep her talking.

"Well, it was always some romantic thing that I saw in the movies. The artsy college student with an old camera sees the world as this beautiful place to explore through the lens. I don't know. I was kind of a loner. Even with my friends, I didn't really feel like I belonged. But, being cute keeps you from being a complete loser."

"Maybe you just needed new friends," Jayce says. I nod in agreement.

"Thanks. Well, I saw this photo of a little boy laughing and it changed my life. His clothes were dirty and torn. Everything around him was ruined. He was skinny and sick looking, but he was laughing anyway. It wasn't a staged laugh. It was genuine. You could feel it in your gut, see it through the photo, the way his eyes lit up. When I saw it, I wanted to know; no I needed to know what made a laugh like that come from a boy with nothing. It made me want to discover that light on my own."

"How inspirational," Cass says with a hint of sarcasm.

If Atara notices it, she doesn't say. "When you find something that moves you, you move with it."

Atara and I share a smile. She's insightful in a way that most people older than her are. It intrigues me.

"Jayce?" Atara asks. "What about you?"

"I'd be working so that I could have enough saved for when I headed back to the states. I'd have been convincing my boyfriend to come with me," Jayce says and then shakes his head. "I'd have probably said something like, there's no time like the present. We never know what could happen tomorrow. As much as I liked living in France, America was my home and I missed it. I wanted to go to college back there. I wanted to just strike out on my own far away from my parent's. I was ready to be independent. And... Darren, he would have said, my love, I'll follow you anywhere, but only after you clean the dishes you left in the sink. He was such a romantic."

Jayce looks like he just was told that all the puppies in the world have disappeared, that someone blew up all the stars, or that Santa Claus never existed. Once again, the raw pain just looks so wrong on him.

I put my hand on his arm and squeeze. He looks at me and places his hand over mine. Cass catches it and raises an eyebrow. Somehow, she makes me feel guilty and I remove my hand.

"So, do you two like each other or something? Or, is this one of those, I'm hurting, you're hurting, so let's just use each other type of situation?"

"Despite what you may have been led to believe, that's not my thing. I like Jasmine as a friend. Besides, I'm almost eighteen. She's thirteen."

"Well, we're all dead, so I don't know if those age rules still apply. Will you still see her as thirteen ten years from now?" She keeps pressing.

I don't like the way she's talking to me, as if it's an interrogation. I'm not the enemy here. I'm doing nothing wrong.

"It doesn't matter. I don't like Jayce like that and he doesn't like me. Boys and girls can just be friends," I defend.

"Is it because he likes boys and girls? I know a lot of people that won't date a guy that, you know, likes to suck-,"

Atara interrupts. "Whoa, Cass. I think you're kind of being rude here. Those aren't questions that you ask."

"Well, if no one asks, how are we supposed to know?" She shrugs as if it's the most obvious thing in the world. It doesn't matter if those questions make other people uncomfortable.

"Well, you were being kind of a bitch about it. Do you have an issue with what I like to suck on, whether it's a guy's or a girl's?"

"No, no issue at all. I just don't like how you flirt with Dorian and now her. Actually, I don't like how you flirt with anybody."

Huh?

"Is that what this is about? You have a crush on Dorian, don't you?" Jayce asks, voice raised. Atara looks away in disappointment and Cass's eyes light up in anger.

"I do not!"

"Then why are you so worried about it? Or, would you rather I flirt with you?" He leans forward, getting closer to her face.

Her eyes narrow in anger.

"Jasmine, we never got to hear your answer about what you'd be doing right now." Atara smoothly changes the subject. She's clearly the peacemaker. Or, she just doesn't want to hear about any crushes that her possible crush may have.

That's understandable.

I play along while Jayce and Cass glare at each other. I'm completely expecting little lightning bolts to crackle between the two of them. "Well, I was thinking about asking my dad if he knew any good modeling agencies to try to get into. My dad did security for plenty of the top agencies whenever they had events, so it wouldn't hurt to ask. I wanted to do runway shows. My sister and I both dance, so I was going to try to make some steps with her and post them on YouTube. Then, there's this boy, Justin, that I wanted to hang out with. Oh, and I wanted to do some volunteer work at the local shelter." I could go on and on about things that I could have been doing. It's hard to stop once I get started. There's just so much that I wanted to do.

They all stare at me and I snap back out of my daydream.

Cass finally asks, "So, just how rich were you?"

◊◊◊

Imagine if you could take your wealth with you when you died, how much greedier people in the world would be. When we were talking about my family's wealth, the way their eyes lit up, made me humbled to realize just how much I had. I never really comprehended just how different my life was in comparison to other people my age. Maybe I just didn't care.

I should have done more to help other people less fortunate while I was alive. I thought that I had more time. Now my conscience doesn't seem so clear.

"Focus!" Micah says to me as Atara tries to land a punch to my face. I've been spacing out for a while now as I think about how unlike my childhood my new friend's lives were.

Atara's fierce as she tries to land multiple well placed shots. I've been dodging and blocking, her speedy attacks, unable to go on the offensive. I'm also not trying my hardest either. Still, she's like a gazelle. The guides are trying to get a feel for our skill levels so that they know where to start. As much as I'm getting yelled at, Micah must not be very happy with my show.

Just as I resolve to focus more, they call us off and tell us to bow. Panting, we bow to each other and turn to Kenji as he nods at each of us and then tells us certain individual things that we need to work on. Keep your guard up, stop telegraphing punches, stop swinging so wildly, anticipate moves, and focus.

Micah gives me a pointed look at the last one. I frown at him. He frowns back. Hey, at least I refrained from rolling my eyes.

"I'm going to work with you on defense. Dorian will handle the offense. Now, step across from your soul guide and we shall begin." We all step forward so that we're three feet away from our partners. "There's another thing; we practice how we play. We are soul tamers. We don't go easy on each other."

Jayce and I glance at each other, Atara gulps, and Cass smirks. Great, just great. I gaze into Micah's dark eyes and feel his energy mix with mine. I can do this. He won't hurt me. Kenji shows us a high guard stance with our dominant leg slightly bent and in front of the other and what's called an "x" block. When he says 'go,' they all strike.

I get my block up in time, but his strength breaks through and his fist hits me in my face. I hit the ground as pain racks through me. If I were alive he'd have probably broke my nose. I look up at him with wide eyes ready to tell him that I quit.

Get up, Jasmine," he orders. His voice is cold and authoritative. It's the voice of a warrior. His command is absolute. At this moment, Micah doesn't look like a seventeen-year-old boy. His true years gleam in his dark eyes.

I look to the others, and they've fared no better. Jayce is rubbing his shoulder, Atara just moved completely out of the way, and Cass is touching her lip and looking at her fingers as if she expects it to be gushing blood. I stand and wipe myself off, my heart beating much faster now.

"Again!" Kenji cries.

We block a little better this time, but not much. The force of Micah's punch jars my body. In panic and anticipation, I block the next one too early and leave myself open to another strike. I hit the ground again.

"Again."

His blows get no softer. My arms are shaking.

"Again."

I grit my teeth against the force and do my best to blink back tears. I don't know if I want to do this.

"Again."

Over and over we do this dance, switching and learning new blocks, switching guides and learning to block their strength or their speed. Then, once I feel that I can no longer even stand, they turn up the juice, throwing combos, increasing their speed, making us choose which blocks would work best.

I can't even recall how many times I hit the ground. But, each time, I force myself to get back up and push. Lying down and crying won't solve anything. I'm a Whitmore. We always find a way. I just have to remind myself what I'm doing it for. We work for two hours straight before we get our first break. It's over far too quickly.

Dorian steps up with a crooked smile. He is far too excited about this. So is Cass, again. Well, we all have our interests, I guess. Dorian looks over all of us for a few minutes, pacing back and forth. Eventually, I begin to fidget under his gaze. That seems to satisfy him.

"I'm going to assume you all know how to punch and kick. Of course, we will go over variations of each, but what I'm going to teach you is how to focus your energy to make your attacks even stronger. Now, let's get started."

Micah steps forward to be the test subject. He turns to face Dorian who bows to him. Micah bows back and then takes a defensive stance.

"The same energy that you feel inside when you travel is the same type of energy you are going to pull from your middle." He gestures to his torso, near his diaphragm. "You'll feel it in your stomach if you focus. It feels like a candle has been lit inside of you, but it won't hurt. That will grow. It will feel like life, like it's the power that you should have had all along. Once you find it, it's yours. It will be easy to have it flow through you. Then, you use it as an extension of yourself. Like this."

Dorian punches directly at Micah's chest, stepping into the blow, remaining perfectly balanced. Micah blocks it, but we all still feel the force of the punch. Micah slides back a few feet, but is no worse for wear. Jayce and I share a look as he raises his hand.

"Uh, how come you didn't teach us how to use our power while blocking?" Jayce asks. He rubs his arms. "It woulda saved us a lot of pain."

"We didn't want you focusing too hard on the power instead of the techniques. With offense, we have a bit of leeway. Less chance of being hurt and as I said, techniques can be refined."

"What does happen if we're hurt during battle, or if we…die?" Atara asks.

"Well, we may still feel as if we're alive, but we aren't, not really. We've been given a special in-between status. But, we're beings of spirit and energy. Demons, spirits, and even other soul tamers can attack and harm us because they are all made basically the same. If we are killed, our souls will move on completely," Gwyn explains.

"So, what's to stop us from growing tired and simply killing ourselves?" I ask.

"A few have," Dorian says.

"But, most of us choose to follow our calling," Micah adds.

"What about rogue soul tamers? Does anyone just sometimes snap?" Cass asks.

The question is met with silence. They all stare at each other as if expecting someone else to respond. In turn, we all shift uncomfortably. Finally, Kenji sighs and lifts his head up.

"We may be special, but we are all still human. Sometimes, the job is too much even for us to bear. Then, they must be dealt with swiftly, for the safety of everyone."

More silence.

"Alright, you slackers. Let's get back to work. I want to feel that power raging inside of you," Gwyn tells us loudly, knocking us out of our funk.

There's a lot more to the soul tamer business than we thought. There's plenty more that they don't really want to reveal to us yet.

"You heard the lady. Start punching and make it good," Dorian commands.

Jayce rolls his eyes and I shrug. We all start punching, trying to breathe and feel our power. Of course, Cass achieves her power punch first. Dorian looks at her with pride.

"Take note, she just set the bar for you lot. Time to catch up."

Surprisingly, Atara is the next to figure it out. She's like Jekyll and Hyde when it comes to this stuff.

So timid on the outside, but beneath the surface when we're sparring, there's something lying in wait, dying to be released. She kind of scares me.

Then it hits me. Oh no, I will not be last this time. I grit my teeth and try to picture a storm brewing inside of me, ready to rip free. I punch Micah as hard as I can. My punch connects and Micah ends up flying helplessly through the air and landing on his back about ten feet away. Everyone else freezes and looks at me. Micah groans and rolls to his side.

Slack jawed, Jayce says, "Well, I'll be damned. That wasn't the punch of a delicate flower. I think you need a new nickname."

"And I think you need to hurry and catch up," Dorian jabs.

"Oh, you wound me." He clutches his heart.

"Keep it up and I'll have Jasmine punch you."

Kenji snorts as Gwyn helps Micah up.

"Shall we switch partners now?" Micah asks.

By the time we come to a stopping point, I feel like I ran three triathlons forward and backward. But, I still have to do the meditating thing with Micah. It'll probably be me more sleeping than truly meditating if I have my way. Just as we say our goodbyes, Cass jogs over to me, not a hair out of place. It sort of pisses me off. Over her shoulder, I see Atara glancing at us.

"Hey."

"Hey," I say back. "What's up?"

"We should work on some things after we meet with our guides. We could go to the roof."

The idea of any more training makes me cringe, but I feel like this is a rare opportunity to hang with Cass. "Um, sure. Maybe we could ask Atara to come too," I suggest.

Cass looks back at her and Atara looks away quickly. "Oh, um, I was hoping it could be just us. I don't want anyone holding us back."

"Well..." I look around. "We can this time, but we're a team. We don't want any of us to fall behind."

"I guess you're right. But, this time, let's just hang out, you and me."

"What happened between you two?" I ask quietly. Curiosity has struck again.

She frowns and thinks about it. "She just rubs me the wrong way. I don't know. Can we just do this, please?" she asks growing irritated.

"That's fine, Cass." I smile.

"Thanks."

She thinks of Atara as the weak link, but I don't see her that way. I'm doing no better than her and neither is Cass. Cass doesn't like to lose. She thinks of me as her competition right now; so, she has to try and test me. I get it. I can be competitive too. We'll just see how this goes.

I'm left alone staring up at the sky. The clear, perfect sky. But, right now, I don't want perfect. I want some clouds, birds flying across the sky, sounds of a city. I want home.

Micah walks over to me interrupting my thoughts and puts a hand on my shoulder. "You did well today. I have a treat for you. Follow me." He disappears and I quickly follow.

We end up in a world that I've never seen before. It feels like summer in the West Coast. I look around expecting to see a beach, but all I see is clear blue skies and a sun that I could reach out and touch because it's so close.

"Where are we?" I ask.

He smiles again. "This is my home. I wanted to show you where I stay."

This time, I look around more slowly. I see movement in the distance- animals. Birds sing and fly above us. Through the trees, I think I see deer. I even hear laughter of children.

"How?"

"Animals have souls too. They live among us in many planes. Not all. I told you that souls move on; well, this is one of those places. This is where I've chosen to stay, to watch over them. There are a lot of children here, some families. It just reminds me of home. There are even places that look like cities. Soul tamers protect those as well."

"Is that a park?" I look off to my right at what looks like a set of slides and swings.

"It is. There's plenty to do around here and the residents have no worries as long as we keep them safe. They don't fear. They don't feel stress or pain the way a mortal would. It is their instinct to fear demons and dark spirits, but there is no need for the pain they felt when they were alive. That's the point of the otherworld, to transcend beyond that. But, they don't reach these safe zones unless they accept what happened to them."

I think about where my parents might be and if they're missing me too. What if they don't even remember? What if they're not even in a place like this?

"Do they keep their personalities?"

"Yes. But, the negative emotions just don't really have a place here."

It sounds kind of zombie-ish to me, but I guess I can understand. It's the whole concept of better place. No suffering.

"Jasmine?"

"Hmm? I'm fine. Show me your home."

Micah pulls me in close and we travel once again. This time, we're standing in the middle of a large room. I look around to find pictures on the wall. Surprised, I step forward to scan the photographs of Micah and his family. I stop at the group photo.

He and his brothers look nearly identical except that they're slightly taller and have shorter hair. All three of them are dressed in polo shirts and slacks. His mother has on a conservative dress. Long sleeves, high neckline, plain yellow. Her hair is tied in a brown bun and she smiles happily as her boys surround her. His father has on a pressed white dress shirt and a yellow tie. He stands behind everyone, towering over them. His hair is cut short as if he spent some time in the military. His beard is clean shaven and makes him look older than he probably is. But, it also makes him look more handsome than he probably looked without.

The other photos are various candid shots. I reach out and touch the edge of one longingly.

"I uh, stole those in a moment of weakness, but it was worth it. I had to use magic to preserve it or it would have disappeared."

I nod in understanding. Micah's not as straight and narrow as I thought. I look around some more. He has other objects on the walls. They look like artifacts that an archeologist would dig up. There are masks that look over a thousand years old, probably made from animal bones. I'm afraid if I touched one it would fall apart. He also has texts that are rolled up like scrolls with thread wrapped around them. Probably things that he's collected. There's a lot of green around. Pillows, accents, etc. He also has a lot of candles. It smells very foresty in here. It's nice and relaxing. Very Micah-like.

It takes me a few minutes to realize that all the items I looked at were on a bookshelf and that he has a fireplace. And a living room. And a whole house. I peek my head around the corner and down the hallway. Is that a kitchen? Why would he need a kitchen?

"You can have a place like this too one day. It's nice to have your own. Gives you something to look forward to." He steps closer and the room gets smaller.

"So, what else were you trying to show me?" I ask, suddenly feeling like a girl at home with a boy whose parents are gone.

He smiles. "There's a soul for us to deliver." Then, he motions for me to follow him before he disappears.

We end up standing in front of an old woman that's looking around, confused, right up at the orange-red sky. We're standing in the middle of nothing, literally. It's like where I awoke. The sky may have some color, but everything else is white and bright. Almost too bright.

Wrapped in a light pink robe, house shoes, and a shower cap, she shuffles around like she's used to having trouble moving. Her body doesn't know that there's no pain here. We approach from her left side, Micah's sword now attached to his back. "Look out for dark spirits lurking," he orders. My eyes scan the perimeter, but everything looks clear.

"Anna, you've done well. It's time for you to go home now."

She looks at Micah, scrutinizing everything about him. She probably had a sharp mind when she was alive. I'd say she was a high school science teacher. "You're not an angel."

He chuckles. "No ma'am, I'm not. But, I am a friend." He extends his arms and steps forward. Slowly, she steps into his embrace. "Don't be afraid. Things will be better now." As he hugs her, her body begins to glow and then she disappears in a haze of yellow sparkles.

Suddenly, he turns, sword drawn with incredible speed. His katana impales a mass of swirling dark energy and then it explodes sending shrapnel of black dust everywhere. I jump back, covering my face.

"It's fine, Jasmine. Just a dark spirit."

"But, she was already gone."

"It wanted to catch us off guard. Sure, it could feast on the spirit of a normal human, but it could control a soul tamer, take our body and make it its own."

"Oh."

"That's why meditation is important too. We need strong minds for the things we do."

I nod. "Do you have to hug them to get them to pass? How did you know her name?"

"No, all it takes is a touch and desire to help them move on. When we track souls, it just happens. We get their names and locations. We can even speak their language. These are gifts given to us by the Soul Kings to make our jobs easier."

"Well, that was sweet of you."

He would blush if he could. "I try. I mean, that's someone's grandma." Micah's eyes flash white and he pauses. It's another otherworldly message. "Come on. There's another one and we need to move fast. They're afraid." He disappears again and I follow.

As soon as I reappear, Micah yells for me to block. I turn just in time to ward off a punch from a small, scaly demon. The beast resembles a dragon. It turns its red reptilian eyes toward Micah and then me. He chooses me as Micah finishes sending the soul away. My body shakes as claws slice inches from my face, followed by teeth snapping at my forearm.

I think of our traveling training and disappear a safe distance away as Micah sends a hard punch into its jaw as he unsheathes his weapon and splits the beast in half. Seconds later, it disappears in a wisp of black smoke. That was close.

"You did well. You stayed calm," Micah compliments while assessing my body for damage. Satisfied, he says, "That's enough for today."

"Thanks."

"You lead the way this time."

I pause for a second, ready to protest that I can't do it, but then, I nod. I return home to my room. Micah joins me a fraction of a second later.

"You're going to make an amazing soul tamer, Jazzy. Your family would be proud."

I smile. "Thanks, Micah." We hug and then he disappears, leaving me alone in my room. I close my eyes and sigh, changing into some shorts and a tank so I can train with Cass even though all I want to do is sleep.

I go to the roof to find her already there waiting on me in some gray sweats and a royal blue compression shirt. Her long hair is braided and lying against her chest. She looks as if she's already been training.

"Hey," I say with a wave.

"What's up? Are you ready?" she asks.

No small talk then. "Sure. Where should we start?"

"Let's uh, work on focusing our energy into our attacks. We can strike these things over here." She points to the dummies to the left of us. They look like normal dummies, but Micah told me that they light up depending on how much power you're using. They are also designed to absorb our attacks without being destroyed so easily.

"I think blue is the highest. Red, green, and blue. Let's try to get five green in a row and at least two blue."

"Sure. Let's do it." I get into my favorite stance which is a mix between one we recently learned and one my dad taught Rayne and me. My feet are shoulder width apart right foot slightly in front, knees bent, weight balanced. My right arm's elbow is pointing inward, my thumb tucked in, and other fingers extended. My left hand is lower in a fist.

Cass is in a low stance, front right knee bent and left leg extended to the side and both arms up in fists.

We both channel our power and then strike. Hers lights red and mine green. I watch her scowl and hit again. It goes green and she smirks in satisfaction. We both hit red next. Well, I hit red so she won't feel bad. That just makes her angry.

"I know you're stronger than me or something. You know how to use your power, so don't hold back on my account. I need to know how far behind you I am."

"I'm sorry. I just don't want this to turn into some bitter competition."

"We'll make each other better and in turn, save a lot of lives. That's why I want this, Jasmine. I want to go back to the world and kill dark spirits that are using people. Dark spirits inhabit the bodies, they kill people and then leave the person to deal with the fallout. Rapists, murderers, serial killers..." As her voice trails off, she turns to the dummy with a scream and strikes it. Her power pushes me back and I look on, mouth open as Cass's body glows white. The dummy glows blue.

"Do you want to talk about it?" I ask as her body returns to normal.

"I made dumb mistakes that cost me my life. I pride myself on my intelligence and stupidity got me killed. I suffered. I'm the reason he was finally caught, but he could have hurt someone else." She peers into the distance.

"Do you have nightmares? Because I know I do."

She turns her back on me. "Let's get back to work."

I turn back to the dummy without another word. If she wants to drop it, I'll let her. Blue, blue, blue, green, green, blue. Each strike gets her attention. Each show of power blows against her clothes. I turn and smile. "You've got some catching up to do."

She snorts and gets back to business. I understand that this is her therapy. I'll be a good friend and team player by just being there. If that is what she needs, I can do this much.

Chapter Ten

*W*e've been traveling nonstop for the past twenty minutes, hopping from world to world, and I am thoroughly exhausted. But, if the excited gleam in Micah's eyes is any indication, we're just beginning. I may be more powerful, but Jayce seems to have the most stamina. He's barely breathing hard. I roll my eyes at him, but he just looks confused.

"Now that we're all warmed up, it's time to finally manifest your weapons. Every soul tamer has a weapon. Some have two. Rarely, a tamer can call upon three, but it does happen. Our weapons are designed to protect us from the evil that we face and give us distinct combat advantages. The type of weapon that you manifest will most likely determine your fighting style. For instance, I am a close ranger fighter. With my katana, it is what I excel at. But, that doesn't mean I stop working on my other skills." Micah outstretches his arm and his blade shimmers into existence.

"We can kill demons and dark spirits with them. We can even cut through a human's physical body and drive out a dark spirit without harming the humans. Our weapons are an extension of us and we must master them in order to be successful." Micah turns and swings at Kenji, but he's wearing two clawed gloves-gauntlets I think they're called. He blocks Micah's attack.

They nod to each other and then Gwyn and Dorian step forward. With a smirk, Gwyn's weapon appears in her hand. It's a hammer with a handle that's about two feet long, has a wide square flat side and a spiked, curved end on the other. It looks heavy and I can just imagine her making her enemies go splat under her assault.

Blood Fox.

Dorian's weapon makes him look like a modern grim reaper. He has a double-bladed scythe. On each end of the staff, the slightly curved blades shine brilliantly. I imagine admiring the beauty of the contrast of the black staff and silver metal right before it slices into you.

"So... Let's begin, shall we." With that, they all attack us at once.

My eyes go wide as Micah's katana nearly slices me in half, followed by a strike from Gwyn. They're not giving us any time to do anything but react and that's all we can do to avoid getting maimed. I can't even look to see how my team is doing. How do I even get my weapon to manifest?

"Damn," I hear Jayce hiss. "You guys really aren't playing games."

"Call your weapons!"

"How?"

Cass fights back, but it really isn't helping. She's getting pushed back and every time she tries to travel, they're right behind her. Dorian cuts through her shirt and I flash to help. I grab her and we disappear. Both of us feel the slice of our flesh as he cuts us. For the first time since meeting them, I feel genuinely afraid of death. They may not mean to, but they could kill me. The thought makes me freeze and Gwyn flies at me from above, hammer raised.

"Jasmine!" Atara calls. But, it's Jayce that saves me.

With a shout, he stands in front of me, arms raised, a glowing staff in his hands. He blocks her attack, but it brings him to his knees.

"You're welcome," he grunts. I snap back to reality.

"Thanks Jayce."

"What? No Casanova?"

"Cool it, playboy."

We smile at each other, but Dorian breaks up the moment.

"We're not finished yet!" He kicks Jayce across the ground and begins to attack again.

We dodge and try to focus, but no one else manifests their weapons for a good five minutes. Cass and Atara release theirs at the same time. Cass has a pair of sais and Atara has a pack of arrows on her back with a bow in her left hand.

"And then there was one."

"What are you waiting for?"

"Ugh!" I whine. "Give me time."

"How about..." Micah taps his lips. "How about we all attack her."

"What?" I look around quickly.

"Now!"

They all really attack me.

I try to dodge and spin, disappear and block, call for my weapons, but I just end up being knocked around. Tears of frustration begin to well up in my eyes, but I don't stop trying.

Atara shoots an arrow at me and it embeds in my shoulder. I cry out in pain and pull it out. It heals quickly, but the phantom pain causes me to bite my lip to endure it. Another arrow, a slash of metal claws, the sing of a katana.

I must do it. I have to do it now. I swing out with both arms; power engulfs my limbs and shoots out to my hands.

My hands tingle and I feel something growing inside of them. It's solid and it feels right. Everyone flies back and I'm crouched on one knee, eyes forward. Slowly, I turn to see what kind of weapons I wield. It has a handle that I'm gripping. They're large "D" shaped with six spikes on the tips and two long ribbons with symbols on them. As I stare, it takes me a second to realize that they're fans. Combat fans.

I swing them as a test and wind blows from my swing. The ribbons are red and the symbols glow white. The handle is metal and the fans are covered in white and red intertwining vines. It's beautiful. I close the fans and find that the hard metal now surrounds the fans, creating another weapon. Long and short range weapons; I have my work cut out for me.

Everyone else is finally inspecting their own tools and our guides let us do so in silence. Cass inspects her sais. Three sharp points with a light blue handled grip; simple and deadly. She swings them and it seems to hum. She tests the weight by throwing them gently in the air with a satisfied nod.

Atara pulls her arrow from her purple sheath as if she's been doing it for years. The movement is smooth, practiced. The tips of the arrows are black, but shine like diamonds are embedded in them. Some have white symbols on the side like my ribbons. The bow itself is strung tightly and I know that it will probably never break. The handle, upper, and lower limbs are a stunning purple too. She shoots one and it cuts through the air with the grace of a swan and the precision of an eagle. She smiles and Gwyn winks at her.

With a pout, Jayce runs a hand along his staff. It's about the length of his body and I can tell from here that it's heavy. He's going to need that stamina of his to master it. Jayce was hoping for a sword or a type of blade, but I think the staff fits him. It's made of a dark brown wood with yellow lightning bolt accents. Using a low stance, he strikes the earth with it and the ground shakes. Finally, he shrugs and places one end on the ground, holding it straight up.

Finally, Micah steps forward. "Congratulations everyone. You're one step closer to being a soul tamer. Each of you will be able to channel a certain element as well. Not everyone can, but we know you will, that's part of the reason why we were all chosen to be your guides. Jasmine, it seems that air is yours and Jayce, you have earth. You two, I'm not sure about."

Atara squints and pulls another arrow. With a slow breath, she sets up another shot. Eyes closed, focused. She releases it like a primal instinct. The arrow cuts through the air and then lights up from the symbols before bursting into flame.

Well, there you have it.

"I would get the element that killed me. I'm terrified of fire now," she admits. Micah steps forward and places a hand on her shoulder.

"We control fire, it does not control us. I will help you conquer that fear, Atara." He smiles at her as she looks up at him with her beautiful gray eyes.

"Thank you," she says quietly.

He nods and then turns to Cass. "This doesn't automatically mean that you control water. But, you guys are special and water is a rare element to control. Water is life. It's purity To manipulate it, you must be able to pull it through the world around you. Still, it would make sense that someone on this team would control it and that each of you would all have a separate element."

"What about you guys?" Jayce asks.

"Well, I control fire. Dorian has air, Gwyn is earth, and Kenji controls air and water."

"How?"

Kenji steps forward. "I discovered it on a mission. But, these separate gauntlets help me control each of the elements. I do not really know how. I just accept that I have been blessed with these gifts and do so humbly. Unlike the others, I can only use the elements with my weapons. They can all call their gifts without help from their tools."

"Dorian will work with you later to see. If you do command water, it just takes time for it to reveal itself.

Don't think that you're falling behind, girly," Gwyn tells her.

Cass clutches her sais tightly, holds her head down and then nods.

"Hey, maybe we can go to the lake together later. It may help you to be around the element," Atara suggests.

"Maybe," Cass responds coolly.

"Okay, back to work. I need you guys to conceal your weapons and then manifest them again until it feels familiar. To get rid of them, imagine them being absorbed by you. After all, you are one with your tools." Micah calls for his blade and makes it vanish repeatedly. "Then, you will need to learn control. Utilizing our elements isn't always necessary and can be dangerous to our allies if we behave recklessly, so we need you all to know when to go all out and when to hold back and rely on your teammates."

Gwyn steps forward with her hammer. She slams one foot on the ground and a piece of earth pops up. With a swing, she sends it sailing into the air like a batter hitting a homerun. "Power and control are important. Being strong is wonderful, we all want that, but how you wield that power, how you analyze situations is what will give you victory. Power doesn't mean success. Remember that," Gwyn says.

"Control your weapons. Reach for them." Micah watches carefully, telling us to relax when needed, encouraging us when we do well. Then, they add traveling to the mix and we jump from place to place, manifesting our weapons as quickly as possible and then banishing them before we can follow our guides to other planes. We learn the energy of the other guides and our friends, switching who we follow as they tell us. They want us to react on instinct, to perceive, evaluate, and act as quickly as possible.

Atara does the best. Her speed is the most superior. Cass is the slowest, but it is not the speed of someone that isn't catching on. It is the speed of someone that is watching and learning beyond the rest of us. She seems to sense things around us that we don't.

The guides then have us defend ourselves with our weapons. We learn when to push our power, when to go on the offensive, and when to hold back. It's challenging and tiring. I end up with many bumps and bruises and being chastised for using too much power.

"Be careful, Jasmine," Dorian warns. "You'll easily destroy everything in your path, even the souls you are seeking to help. You must listen to your body and strengthen your mind."

I nod. "I'll do better."

"Good. I will help you," he promises.

"There's something big that we're going to have to be a part of very soon isn't there? Maybe I'm wrong, but our training seems fast and intense," Jayce says, stepping next to me.

"Things are changing around here. Spirits are getting stronger. Demons are breaking free more frequently. You all just need to be ready. When we need you to step up, you need to be prepared. Focus only on getting better for now," Kenji says.

We all look at each other, accepting that we won't get more out of them anyway.

"Jasmine, I want you and Atara to pull your weapons. We need to show you what those symbols are," Micah says.

We both comply and Micah steps back and allows Kenji to get closer. He reaches for one of Atara's arrows and runs a hand along it. With a whisper, it lights up and he pulls a symbol free the way you would a sticker. It's on a long strip of paper.

"These are seals. They are meant to disorient or bind spirits and demons. Jasmine, you have the same symbols on your ribbons. Both of you can hold stronger opponents that you are having trouble defeating or send an enemy back to where they came from without killing them."

"For Jayce and Cassandra, it is still possible for you to bind an opponent, but it will be more difficult as you will have to memorize the symbols and recite an incantation. Jasmine and Atara are just more spiritually aware and that's okay. We all have our gifts."

"Basically, we kind of suck," Jayce says.

"Oh, don't be like that," I say. "I think we're all pretty awesome."

"Says the girl with the weapons that you can use about six different ways."

"Jayce-,"

"It's alright, Jazzy. We all knew that you were going to be special. After all, why else would they kill you so soon?"

"Seriously?" Cass rolls her eyes. "You're not pouting, are you? If you think that you suck, one, don't include me in that, and two, do better."

Dorian chuckles. "Cass is right. Your weapons choose you for a reason. There is more to that staff you wield. You have to pay attention." He leaps at Jayce with his scythe and Jayce curses as he calls for his staff. Dorian toys with him a bit as Jayce grows more and more angry. He swings wildly and misses Dorian by a couple of feet. Dorian disappears and puts him in a chokehold as he reappears behind him.

"Calm down, boy. You're no longer fighting smart."

"I don't want to be weak," he rasps.

"And you're not." Dorian lets him go and Jayce falls to the ground. He stays on his hands and knees clutching at the earth.

"Each of you will surpass us in no time because each of you were born to be something new. Don't be afraid to push and rely on each other. You're all incredible. Yes, we're pushing you, but you're handling it better than you realize. I think I can speak for the boys when I say that you're doing us proud." Gwyn smiles that motherly smile and it makes me miss my own mother.

Kenji helps Jayce up as Micah stares at me.

I'm okay, I tell him in my head.

He nods.

"Pick a partner. You'll spar with no weapons for ten minutes and then you will switch until you've sparred against everyone. Then, we will switch. Gwyn will spar with Cass, Jayce with Micah, Jasmine with Kenji, and Atara with myself. That will be twenty minutes with weapons and twenty minutes without. When you are done, you should all get some rest and then spend some time together. I think that you all need to bond," Dorian says.

I groan. That's a lot of sparring. I'm not going to want to spend any time with them after that. I open my mouth to ask for a rain check when Cass grabs my arm.

She says mockingly, "I know you're not tired, delicate flower."

I narrow my eyes at her. "Don't forget that some flowers have thorns."

Beside me, Micah chuckles. "That's the spirit."

"You better not hold back either," she warns.

"Only if you think you can keep up."

◊◊◊

"Everything hurts," Jayce whines. I grunt in agreement.

We are all floating in the lake, moaning and groaning. Sparring with each other was tiring enough, but our guides had thoroughly kicked our butts. It was embarrassing really. I don't think I even got one kick in.

"I don't know if I can do this," Atara admits.

"We can't quit. It'll get easier," Cass says firmly.

"Well, right now, I want to quit," she responds.

"That makes two of us. We're dead, I shouldn't have to deal with muscle aches," Jayce says with a groan as he floats and bumps against Cass.

"Just imagine though, how powerful we'll end up being."

Just then, there's laughter from the shore. We all turn to stare at two tall strangers. Both guys are shirtless. One has chocolate colored skin with a brush cut, designs on the side of his head, and the other one is Atara's light skin color with short curly hair, black at the bottom and red at the ends. Both of them are cute. And shirtless. And cute.

"Hello," Jayce says since I've seem to have lost my voice.

"What's up, guys?" the curly-haired boy says. He smiles and gazes at all of us.

We swim back to shore and greet the newcomers. Their dark brown eyes shine in appreciation and I bite my lip. Brush cut notices and so does Jayce with a raised eyebrow. I ignore him.

"We haven't seen you around here yet. You guys must be the new team. I'm Adrian and this is Christian," curly hair says.

"Yeah, they decided to add us to a team too. We're going to be guarding important gates if there's high levels of demonic activity. What are you going to do?"

"They uh, haven't told us yet," Atara admits.

Cass eyes the two with a frown. She doesn't like that they know and we don't.

"Huh, that's weird. I thought they'd tell you by now since you guys are apparently the prototypes."

"They'll tell us when we're ready," I say.

"And we've introduced ourselves, but we didn't catch your name," Christian says.

"I'm Jasmine, but you can call me Jazzy. This is Atara, Cass, and Jayce."

"So, where are your other people?" Cass asks.

"They're just hanging out alone. Lena and Erin. They wanted some girl time."

"How old is everyone?" Jayce asks.

"Well, I'm seventeen, Christian is fifteen, and both girls are sixteen. What about you?" Adrian asks.

"I'm fifteen too. Jayce is seventeen, Cass is fourteen, and Jazzy's thirteen."

"Thirteen? Ouch."

"Hey!"

"Right. It doesn't change how cute she is," Christian says with a smile.

I blush and Jayce coughs, nudging me.

"Thank you," I say, quietly.

"All of you are cute, actually."

"All of us?" Jayce asks, playfully. He's such a flirt.

"Come on, man, we're strictly for the ladies. But yeah, you're a good-looking guy. Captain of the soccer or baseball team type. You're too skinny to be a quarterback, ya know. But yeah, Lena's guide might go for a guy like you. He's nineteen. Name's Mateo. I'll introduce you if... you girls hang out with us sometime."

"What do you do for fun?" I ask. Cass and Atara both just look uncomfortable. It's like they've never made conversation with a random person before.

"Well, sometimes we jump and search for dark spirits. Sometimes we hide objects from each other and use clues to find them. Or, we just come up with new games and stuff based on our powers."

"You're allowed to search for spirits on your own?"

"Well, what our guides don't know won't hurt them," Christian winks. Flirt. He's like the straight version of Jayce.

"And what happens if you get put in a situation you can't handle?" Cass asks, arms crossed.

"Gee, mom, you sound like the other girls."

"Hmm, where are they? They sound like they've got some sense."

"Chill out, girl. We're not yours to worry about. But, if you want to come with us on a hunt, you are welcome to it," Adrian tells her.

"Cass is just concerned. Dark spirits are no joke," Atara defends.

"Alright, we'll chill out," Christian says.

"How would you know how dark spirits are?" Adrian asks.

"Well, Jazzy's seen a demon or two and Cass and her guide killed a dark spirit a couple of days ago."

"You did?" I ask, turning my head quickly. "Why didn't you tell me?"

"Well, I didn't know I needed to."

I roll my eyes.

"What?" she asks.

"It's just that I told you about my encounters and you've been holding back. I just don't get it."

"It's not a big deal, Jasmine."

"Alright, Cassandra."

"So... where are you guys going?" Jayce asks.

"We were just about to do a little bit of traveling. There's this beautiful world that you can manipulate. Like, if you can imagine something good enough, it'll appear for a couple minutes."

"That sounds dope," I say. "We should go."

"I'm down," Jayce says.

Cass and Atara look at us, but Cass just shrugs.

"They did say bond," Cass reasons.

"Uh, I don't know if I'm really comfortable with that," Atara admits.

"What's wrong? You don't trust us? We're on the same side."

"I don't know you. I don't just see a cute guy and jump up and do whatever they ask. That's just not me," Atara says defensively.

Is that what she thinks I'm doing?

"It isn't even like that. But, suit yourself. I'm not gonna beg, no matter how cute you are either," Christian responds, and still manages to sneak in a flirty comment. He's a flirt ninja.

She rolls her eyes. "Look, I'm not trying to be a bitch about it. I've just never been that girl. Don't take it personally."

"I get it. It's okay. Maybe next time. What about the rest of you?"

"Well, I can stay with Atara if you two want to go," I say.

"What? No, we can all go. We'll be together, Atara. It's not like you're going alone," Jayce reasons.

"You're just using us so you can meet a boy. You are so going to owe me," she says.

Jayce grins and bumps her. "So, is that a yes?"

"I suppose."

"Well, let's go then." Adrian and Christian touch each of us and take us to this 'incredible new world.'

I blink twice and when my eyes adjust, I find myself staring at beauty which I cannot truly describe.

The sky is littered with stars and four moons. One moon looks like it is about to set while the others seem to dance among the stars in various points of the sky. The light from them paint the earth in eternal twilight. I look down and notice that the ground, covered in a purple, cloudy, haze reminds me of what I imagine star dust looks like.

Eyes wide, I turn to scan the rest of the world. Trees and flowers are painted in fall-like fashion and in the distance, brightly colored cliffs with shimmering waterfalls run down the sides. The beauty is breathtaking and I want to take the time to explore this place sometime soon.

To my left, Christian begins to manipulate the smoky, purple, clouds at our feet. He reaches out and swirls it around his hand and then he pushes it away. A couple seconds later, a car materializes right in front of us.

Jaw dropped, the four of us stare in awe at the silver Mustang in front of our faces. So realistic. Cass reaches out to touch it, but stops just a few inches away. She begins to pull back when Adrian laughs.

"It doesn't bite. Just touch it."

She touches the car and a low whistle escapes her. "Wow."

"I know, right. I've been moving up to bigger things and working on trying to keep them around longer. This is as big as I've gotten."

"Can things move once they've been manifested?" Atara asks, walking around the car. It begins to shimmer and then it finally disappears.

Apparently, the larger items are harder for him to maintain.

"Well, yeah, I think. I haven't tried anything but inanimate objects," he admits.

Atara closes her eyes and then a pair of cats shimmer into existence, mewling and licking themselves. She smiles in triumph as the smoke swirls around them as they move. A few seconds later, they disappear.

Christian and Adrian look at her as if she just grew two heads.

"How did you?"

"Simple."

Jayce smirks at me and then closes his eyes. He creates himself smiling and giving his best beauty pageant wave. I roll my eyes. "It's the meditation."

Cass narrows her eyes at me and we seem to read each other's mind. She closes her eyes first and then I follow suit. I smirk when I hear the rest of them cry in surprise. When I open my eyes, the demon that attacked me when Micah first rescued me is snarling near them. Cass's own dark spirit is swirling around looking menacing.

The facial features are completely distorted. Its jaw is elongated almost comically, its eyes are empty, lifeless pits that one could fall into and remain forever trapped. The spirit hovers in the air, arms and legs stretched at odd angles. It's the stuff of good scary movies, except for, real life.

"What the heck is that?"

"Just things we've encountered," Cass responds.

"That is so cool. Do you think that with our combined power we could make them corporeal?" Atara asks.

"Now you're thinking," I say.

"Wait. Whoa. Can you do that?" Adrian asks.

"Why not? What do you think this world is for? Just for fun and games? I don't think so. It's a place to sharpen certain skills. Think bigger picture."

"If you think you can pull it off, I'm down. It'll be awesome training, especially if we can get them to stay longer than a few seconds," Christian says.

"Alright, let's do it," Jayce says.

"Cass and I will imagine them and the rest of you will focus on making them real. We should probably join our hands and sync our energy."

"Think we can do it?"

"We're soul tamers, right? Hell yeah we can do it."

We all circle up and join hands as Cass and I breathe deeply. I imagine pupil-less eyes, horns, powerful, inhuman bodies, and aggression. Then, I picture three of them while I reach for the familiar feeling of my ally's energy. Christian and Adrian try their best to tune theirs, but it isn't quite working. It's as if they keep hitting the wrong key on the piano.

"Focus. You guys really need to take your meditations seriously. It will strengthen your mind," Jayce tells them.

"That's that weak, boring, girly stuff," Adrian whines.

"But, it's not. Now, if you want to see if this will work, shut up and focus," Cass orders.

"Geeze, okay."

We try again and shortly, I feel the purple smoke swirl around us. I can sense them circling, unsure as if they don't even understand what they are. Then, we all stop as we realize that it worked. That's when they attack.

We break apart and call for our weapons as we dodge slashing claws and gnashing teeth. The smoke dusts up all around us, causing our vision to be obscured. No matter, we can feel their energy. After all, we created them.

I blow one of the spirits into Jayce who slams it into the ground with his staff. Atara shoots one between the eyes and it disappears in a cloud of smoke. Adrian and Christian fight in sync with two tonfa blades and circular bladed weapons that whistle every time Christian swings them.

It's exhilarating and eye-opening how well we all sync with each other. Our adversaries may be bred from our imagination, but they seem as real as any of us. We easily do this dance and defeat all our opponents without breaking a sweat. Our training is paying off.

This is the most alive I've felt since I've been here and I'm extremely sad when it's all over. We did what we did without our guides to help us. It makes me believe in our power.

"Okay, that was pretty dope. You guys are not bad at all," Christian compliments.

"Thank you," we say in unison.

"We've got an early start tomorrow, but we should do this again. I'll see you guys later. Bye, Jazzy," Christian smiles. They both disappear with a wave and Jayce immediately turns to me.

"Bye, Jazzy," he mocks.

I swat him on the arm. "Oh, shut up. He's cute, but I don't even like him like that, yet. I don't even know him."

"They seem…goofy."

"That's a good word to describe them."

"Goofy or not, I want to meet this Mateo. They better keep their word."

"Should we really be thinking about having a love life right now? I mean, there are more important things," Cassandra comments.

"Buzzkill," Jayce whispers, but he can't hide the sadness in his eyes. He just wants to keep his mind off his boyfriend. I get that.

"Come on, let's go back and get some rest. I'm sure that we're going to have a long day tomorrow," Atara says.

I groan. "I don't even want to think about how much more training we'll have to go through."

"Stop being so soft," Cass says.

"Stop pretending like you're not affected."

"Whatever." She takes a deep breath and disappears, leaving us behind.

"Well, what's her problem?" Jayce asks.

"Why don't I go talk to her?" Atara suggests.

"No offense, 'Tara, but Cassie doesn't seem to like you very much," Jayce says honestly and gently.

Atara smiles. "She'll just have to get over it now won't she. She thinks I'm weak, but I'm not. I wouldn't be here if I were. We're a team. She'll come around." Her gray eyes shine with hope and I can't help but to smile at her.

"Atara? Do you have feelings for Cass?" I ask suddenly.

Jayce raises an eyebrow at me as if he didn't expect me to ask her. I didn't really mean to; it just sort of fell out of my mouth. Oops.

Atara looks between me and Jayce before sighing heavily. "Honestly, there are things that I like about her, but I really don't know. I can't say that I really know what it feels like to actually like anyone, boy or girl."

"Can you explain that to me?" I ask. I don't have that experience. I've had plenty of crushes. Jayce nods as if he wants an explanation too.

She bites her lip in contemplation. "Well, I'll see a guy that I like as a friend. I'll think that he's funny and smart, definitely cute, but I don't know if I'd want to kiss him. Or, I'll see a girl like you, Jazzy. Kind, cute, cool, and I'll think that I *should* want to kiss her, but I don't. I don't think I've just ever had anyone that makes me feel any kind of way."

"Sounds complicated and confusing."

"It is. I like her, but I'm not sure what kind of like it is. With her, for some reason, I just want to be close to her and have her accept me. I don't feel that's what liking someone means though."

"Maybe not for you. It's okay to ask yourself those questions. We're pretty young and we should be down there figuring it out, but instead, we're here learning to fight monsters while having teenage feelings and still being very limited with our options," Jayce says.

"Maybe Cass is right. Now isn't the time for love," I say.

"Who said anything about love?" Jayce asks.

"You know what I mean."

"I know what you mean. Maybe after we get a better feel for what we're doing here then there will be possibilities. You shouldn't go searching for love, anyway. If it happens, it happens." Jayce smiles at Atara and turns to me. "So, leave Christian alone."

I snort. "Whatever. He's already forgotten. Now, let's get back so I can get some sleep."

"Now that's a word I love to hear."

◊◊◊

Nearly two weeks pass and the routine is the same. Our team just keeps getting stronger and I must say that I'm excited to see what we're really made of. Today though, I'm going to be working with Dorian.

But, as soon as I finish getting ready, I hear Micah ask to enter my room. I give him the all clear and he materializes right in front of me. His long hair is down and as usual, he's shirtless. I take a second to appreciate his toned form before I give him a smile.

"What's up?" I ask.

"I have news of your sister. It's good news too."

"Well, tell me."

"Your sister has decided to become unmade. She has been marked by the Immortals, a race of warriors that have served humanity in the shadows for millennia. Their power is infused with mankind, thanks to a powerful spell created by their king. I'm told that when Alexander bonded his energy with the humans, there were about thirty thousand humans in existence. That tells you just how powerful he was. Some of his allies assisted him in amplifying his power in order for a piece of his chakra to embed with every human. He fixed the spell so that every person's life force could grow that power into something of their own. Now, she will be able to unlock those powers."

Micah smiles and seems to expect me to jump for joy. But, if I've learned anything, it's that there's always a price. He frowns at my expression.

"What's the bad news?"

"She'll pass, Jasmine."

"Pass what, Micah? How does she unlock that power? Does she almost have to die?" Dying seems to be the key ingredient

"Jasmine…"

"Just tell me what my sister is sacrificing."

"It takes incredible determination to unlock that power. I can't go into detail, but some don't survive."

"She could die?! After everything she's been through, she could still lose her life? No. Send me back; let me talk to her somehow." I start to panic and pace as I make an effort to focus on my sister. It's imperative that I reach her.

"Jasmine, you can't. It is forbidden."

"No! She's doing this because of me, because of what she lost and it's your fault! You and the Soul Kings and whoever else was involved. You did this. I want her to live a normal, long life, not take a risk like that. If she dies, will she come here?"

"No. She isn't chosen to be a soul tamer."

"Then, stop her!" I scream. I accidently unleash a wave of power and Micah grunts as it sends him to his knees.

"Please, Jasmine. Calm down. It's good news, really. If she's strong like you claim, she will succeed. Believe in her."

"I can't take that risk." I begin to cry. "Micah, she's my sister, my only family left alive. I don't want her doing this."

He stands. "It isn't your call. Rayne has chosen her path."

"You bastard. You knew about this days ago and didn't say anything, did you?" Wind begins to swirl around me, commanded by my rage. Before I realize it, my weapons are in my hands.

"Are you going to attack me?" Micah's eyes contain a hint of sadness. "I've been checking up on her for you. I've been breaking rules for you. Is this how you choose to thank me?"

"I look at my fans and the wind dies down. Suddenly, Dorian appears at Micah's side, eyes narrowing as he takes in the situation.

"I don't want my sister to die because she wants revenge. I wasn't even supposed to die yet. This shouldn't be happening."

"But, your parents dying could have set her on the same path."

"No! She would've had me. She would live for me, taking care of me." The wind picks up again. How dare he tell me what my sister would have done. He knows nothing.

"You need to calm down," Dorian commands.

"You don't get to tell me what to do," I growl, unable to control the rage that's consuming me.

Dorian takes a step forward as Micah casts a wary glance between us.

"Stop acting like a child."

"You know nothing about me. You don't even remember what it's like to feel like this. Get out. Both of you. If my sister doesn't make it through this, I blame all of you. I'm not doing any more training until I know for sure she's safe."

"You can't be serious."

"How are we supposed to do that? We can tell you, but you won't believe us."

"Figure it out. Leave." I turn away and stare out the window. Micah places a hand on my shoulder. "Don't. Touch. Me."

He sighs.

Yet, Dorian decides to open his mouth again. "I'd expected more from you."

Tears in my eyes, I turn and go after Dorian, but Micah holds me back with his muscular arms wrapped around my waist. I'm trapped in stone.

"If you were all doing your jobs, you wouldn't have needed me! You're the ones who weren't strong enough. Who's the real disappointment?" I kick and struggle against him, but he's using his power to keep me in check.

Dorian looks at me as if I've slapped him. Maybe he realizes how true my words are. He opens his mouth to respond and thinks better of it. Then, he disappears. Micah finally lets me go.

"Get out, Micah. I don't want to look at you." I turn and walk back to the window. Finally, I feel him leave. Finally, I'm alone. Hot tears fall from my eyes until I fall asleep.

Chapter Eleven

I knock two times before I pop my head inside. It's dark, but I can see her body flip sides. Then, she huffs. I tiptoe into the room and shut the door before making my way to her bed.

"Rayne," I whisper as I shake her gently.

"Mm, what?" her groggy voice responds.

"I can't sleep. I had a nightmare," I whisper a little too loudly.

"Hmm?" she asks again, still a bit out of it.

"Can I sleep with you? I'm scared," I try again.

With some effort, she manages to peek one hazel eye open, but I can tell that she's not seeing me. "Come on." She lifts the cover up for me to slide under and I crawl over her larger body. It takes a couple seconds for me to get comfortable and adjust to the cold temperature of the sheets from the side of the bed that she hadn't warmed. Finally, I close my eyes.

"Jazzy," Rayne mumbles.

"Hmm?"

"I'll always protect you," she promises before she falls back fast asleep.

◊◊◊

The next week passes and my friends try to talk to me, but I send them all away. Jayce was the unhappiest about that, but he'll get over it. I don't have anything to say to any of them. Instead, I've been trying to meditate to find Rayne. Of course, I haven't been successful. It only frustrates me further.

To remain calm, I've begun painting again. Everything so far has been loud and angry clashes of color, but it's helped. I've been able to find a little bit of peace. But, it doesn't completely eliminate the anger festering in the pit of my stomach.

I haven't even left my room because I don't want to risk running into anyone. It's been difficult to stay in one place, but I know how to be stubborn. My whole family were masters at that.

The next evening, I decide to leave my room. Even if it's not real, I need to see them- I need to see my family. I conjure some sweats and a hoodie, pulling the hood over my head before feeling for the resonance of the other world before disappearing. I reform in a cloud of purple smoke that's swirling around me. I create a chair to sit in similar to the one in my dining room. The chair is a dark brown with gold accents on the arms and legs. The back is a soft leather that's more comfortable than it looks. Once I'm sure that I'm strong enough to keep the chair for a long while, I sit and close my eyes.

One of my biggest fears is forgetting their faces. I don't want to ever search my memories and still be unable to recall round, hazel eyes, a big smile and full lips, or long, wavy hair. I don't ever want to forget. Doing this will help me remember.

I start with my mother, picturing her delicate features- heart shaped face, hazel eyes, small lips, flawless skin, slightly pointed nose, and any other feature I can remember. I work the image in my mind, tweaking it and then willing it solid, whole, and as real as I can get it. I feel my power expanding and hugging the mold of my mom I'm forming.

It feels so similar to when I'm working with clay that it comes easily. Then, it clicks and I know that I'm successful. I open my eyes and she's standing before me. Her smile is so familiar that I can't help the tears that spill from my eyes.

Her hair is long and falls just under her chest. She's wearing her favorite pair of diamond earrings that my dad got her for her birthday. Her dress is long and light blue, her favorite color, and she's wearing her favorite shade of light pink lipstick.

"Mom," I whisper as if speaking loudly will break the spell. I run into her arms and surprisingly, she hugs me back. I don't question it, even if this imposter's body doesn't feel as soft and warm as my real mother's. She looks like her right now; that's what matters. She's here and I have the chance to say goodbye.

I pull away and my mom touches my face. I place my hand on top of hers. "Mom, I love you so much and I'm so sorry about what happened to you. I feel like it's my fault. If you would've just gone to the panic room with me, maybe you would have lived. I wasn't going to survive anyway and it seems that you died for nothing."

Her screams pierce through my memories. I shake them away. I don't want to go back to that place. I don't want to remember that fear and pain. Her body begins to flicker and disappear as I lose focus.

"No!" I close my eyes again and solidify her image. "Mom, what you did for me was incredibly brave and selfless. I will never ever forget the sacrifice that you made to protect me. I hope that I can make you proud here, but if Rayne doesn't- I just don't know how I can continue to go on and trust them."

I hang my head low and imagine what my mom would tell me. She'd say that I can't sit back and wait for the past to change. She'd say that I should take what I've been given and try to become a better person with it. I guess in this case, what happens to Rayne is out of my hands. She made her own decision and I can't go back and change her mind. I've been given the opportunity to live- even if it's not the way I could have ever fathomed. I can't just throw that away when there are people counting on me.

Even if I want to continue to blame them.

As I look up, the image of my mom disappears as my father stands before me. He looks at me calmly, waiting to listen as he always does. Even though he's much taller than my tiny frame, having him look down on me isn't usually imposing. It never made me feel small until now.

I frown at him.

He's dressed in stone gray business slacks and a black golf shirt. My dad hardly ever dressed down. I wonder if he had separate clothes for his separate life. His illegal life.

"You killed people and I don't know if I can ever see you the same way. What you did started all this mess, Dad. You created the opportunity. You were doing what you thought was right; but, what I want to know is for who? Was it your pride, your reputation? You've always talked to us like people, not little kids, and I think that's why I understand a lot of what other people my age don't. But this, this I don't understand at all."

I sigh as I look at my father, expecting him to answer me, but he's not my father. He's not really the one that can answer my questions.

"I'll learn to forgive you because I love you. But, you were supposed to protect us and it hurts that you didn't. I'm sure you hate yourself for letting that happen. It's too late to change things. In the short time that I've been here, I've changed though. I speak up and I try not to second guess myself. I'm strong, dad, and I can protect people. It just sucks that the one person that I love most is off limits from my protection. So, I'm asking you to watch over her, and take care of mom too. I'll be okay."

I allow him to disappear in a cloud of smoke. Then, I begin to conjure Rayne, but I stop. Something feels different. I can't put my finger on it, but something isn't right. My body feels like it's on autopilot. I stand there as if I'm in a trance as flashes of death and destruction speed past my eyes. It's a vision. I don't know how I know it, but I'm absolutely sure.

Something is broken- a barrier or a gate. It shatters like glass. Shards of energy fly into the atmosphere and get reabsorbed into sky in violent colors. The action feels angry, vengeful.

Floodgates have opened.

Creatures break through.

Claws, wings, gnashing teeth, ear-piercing and bloodcurdling screams fill every inch of space. It's a sense overload. It smells of rotted flesh, sulfur, and opened bowels. The stench seems to go on forever.

Soul tamers try to fight, but are consumed. They reach the crumbled gate and are swallowed like plankton and krill to a whale. The sheer number of monsters that flood through the divide paralyze some of the warriors with fear. Their final deaths are quick, but brutal.

Entire worlds disappear like dry leaves in an inferno. There are screams. Demons claw their way back to the mortal world through weakened barriers that divide the planes. They shred through them like a knife through wet paper.

Soul tamers are possessed and souls are eaten. I feel it and I see it as if it's happening right now. They call to me, beg me to help, but I'm not strong enough.

I'll never be strong enough.

I fall to the ground as the vision overwhelms me. Then, the world goes dark.

Chapter Twelve

I awake with a gasp, ready to fight whatever entity that comes for me, but to my surprise, it's just a shirtless Dorian that stands before me. After a couple blinks, I realize that I'm in my room. He stands silently by as I compose myself and shake away the fogginess in my mind. I sit up all the way against the headboard and remove myself from under the covers.

"What happened?" I ask.

"I was hoping that you'd be able to enlighten me. Your energy was going crazy and then it just disappeared. We searched for you thinking you'd been harmed."

I put my hand to my head hoping to recall some of my visions. "Well, I saw some things. Scary apocalyptic type things." I shiver.

"Tell me."

"There were demons and worlds being destroyed, soul tamers falling by the dozen. The world went up in an inferno and the mortal world was in danger. It was horrific."

Dorian stares me down and for a few seconds, I don't think he believes me. I'm about to tell him that I'm not making it up when he holds up a hand to speak.

"The Soul Kings gave you a vision. They must think that it's important for you to know and to try to convince you that we can't do this without you, Jasmine Whitmore. You are special and I think that it's time that I tell you exactly why." Dorian gives me a sympathetic look as if he wishes he could have told me sooner.

"Why now and why you? Why isn't my guide telling me this?"

"Just because Micah was chosen to be your personal guide doesn't mean that the rest of us are not your mentors as well. We will all share different bonds and the Soul Kings feel that I will be able to help you the most. They have given me permission to enlighten you about your unique history."

"In other words, what made me disposable." I cross my arms.

"You know what? Get over it. You're dead. It was a necessary evil. None of us took delight in knowing that you were going to die so soon and so brutally. We all mourn for you just as we mourn for every single life lost. But, what you're doing is selfish. Cassandra, Atara, Jayce- they're all waiting on you to come to your senses. If what you say is true, if what you saw in that vision is true, they will all fail without you. All of you together are what's important."

I hold up my hand for him to stop. He's right and I don't want to hear anymore. The truth really does hurt and if I'm being completely honest, that vision is going to give me nightmares.

"One more thing."

"No, I get it. I-,"

Dorian interrupts. "Your sister survived. She has been unmade and is starting on her quest to seek justice for your deaths." He places two fingers on my forehead and an image of Rayne becomes clear in my mind. She cut her hair to look like mine.

She's chained up, the shackles eating into her skin. The image fast forwards to her being beaten, tortured, and healed multiple times. She's unclothed and looks like she's lost all her dignity. But, there is fire in her eyes. Then, the image changes again and Rayne breaks free of her shackles, pulling them from the stone with incredible power. She fights her captor and then collapses. The vision fast forwards again and she's healed and with Selene. Then, the picture fades.

I fall to my knees in astonishment. She did it. Rayne did the impossible and I doubted her. I stopped believing in my big sister and I feel like I betrayed her. I hang my head down in shame as tears fall.

"She has her own journey. You share the same blood and you both have very special legacies to fulfill. Don't worry, Jasmine. The Immortals will raise her up into a fierce warrior. She will fight for the humans in her world while you fight for them here. You will always be connected to her, but if you always worry about what could happen to Rayne, you'll never move on."

"You're right. I was just afraid for her and for myself. I still am. But, they're probably scared too. All I've done is push them away when they've tried to help."

He smiles. "You can make it up to them. We all understand. Just, don't forget that you're never alone."

He helps me up and I wrap my arms around him in a tight hug.

"Thank you, Dorian."

"You're very welcome, Jasmine Whitmore. Now." He walks me to the edge of the bed. "Listen well. All four of you are going to be some of the greatest warriors that we have ever known. As you know, we were all born for this, but you, you have a divine right to be here."

"What do you mean?"

"The world used to be a much different place when people actually believed in the preternatural. They were witnesses to many amazing events as well as horrible atrocities. Even before the Immortal, King Alexander fused his essence with human kind to help protect them, the Soul Kings sought their own solutions to keep the human race from going extinct."

"Alexander is the reason why Rayne could be unmade?"

"Yes. He was one of the most powerful beings in any world and one of the kindest. All humans now carry a piece of his power in their DNA. It lies dormant until the Immortals release it. It has now been unlocked inside of your sister."

"Okay, I understand it a little better now. You can continue."

"A few Soul Kings made a choice that they would be punished for, for over an eon- they mated with human women by disguising themselves as beautiful, nearly perfect men."

"They didn't... rape them, did they?"

"Not physically. It can be argued that it wasn't much different. They chose willing partners, but at the same time did not reveal what they truly were."

"Deception by an angel."

Yes. But, they were desperate and felt that what they'd done was for the greater good. We can debate about the ethics of it another time. Have you ever heard of the term Nephilim?"

"Um, no. What is that?"

"There's great debate among humans about who the Nephilim really are. The term doesn't really fit here because we have different names that we use, but it will paint a picture. People believe that Nephilim are children of humans and angels, sometimes depicted as giants. Others have believed that they were just another type of human or offspring of Neanderthals and modern humans. I've also heard some people push the theory that they were half angel half demon. The most important clue to those that believe is that they were called offspring of 'sons of God' and 'daughters of men.' They were shunned by both good and evil and feared for their power."

"Is that what happened to them, they were outcasts?"

"In a way, yes. They were created for a purpose and yet punished for their father's sins. Those who weep divine blood. We call them abyss walkers or transcendents and you are a descendant of one."

I blink twice. "What?"

"You carry the blood of the Soul Kings inside of you. And, you are powerful."

"But, how after all these generations can I still be that strong? Shouldn't the blood be, I don't know, all bled out?" I can't wrap my head around this. Me? A descendant of an angel?

"Jasmine, I know no other being that is more powerful than an angel. They may be out there, but I have never encountered them. It would take a hundred millennia for that power to run dry."

I stutter, "Wh-which side of my family?" It may be unimportant, but it's the only complete question I can think of right now.

He tilts his head to the side as if he's listening to someone. "Your mother's."

I nod dumbly. "Uh, who was he? The abyss walker, and what happened to him?"

"His name was Hector and he died long ago. He may have lived as an outcast, but he died a hero. You see, abyss walkers were able to travel freely even to the gates of hell to do battle. They could walk the line between each reality despite their mortality. A normal mortal would never survive the punishment of traveling to a land of death. A soul tamer can't hold their physical form in the human world. Abyss walkers can do both. Hector gave his life to close one of the gates keeping a demon named Malphus sealed. His power alone made the gate once again unbreakable. He lived to be two hundred and before he died, fathered three children."

"What about the Soul King? Who is he?" I ask, leaning forward.

"That, I can't reveal. But, I will tell you that the last child of the Soul King was to return home to help stop the war."

"You didn't say anything about a war. Is it going on now?" I ask fearfully. They've been pushing us like crazy and they're experimenting with these teams, but they never mentioned war.

"I don't think it's a war in the way you're imagining. There's always going to be wars between us and those that seek to do harm to humanity. But, something is changing in the mortal world and here. Demons and spirits are growing emboldened. We need a show of force to gain the advantage."

"That's us."

"Correct. We're only going to push you harder and now that you know who you are, I expect you to hold fast to the knowledge that you are the most powerful among us. If you work for it."

I gulp. "What if I fail?"

"We won't let you," Dorian says with such certainty that I think my heart is going to beat out of my chest.

"What about the others? Why are they so special?"

"If you hadn't noticed, Cassandra is growing to be a genius in her own right. Have you ever heard of Marcus Cassius Scaeva?"

"Um, no. Who was he?"

"Long story short, he served under Julius Cesar and was one of his greatest generals. He was known for his loyalty and strength. He was thought to be un-killable because of all the battles that he survived when all seemed lost. He was a machine."

"Let me guess, he's an ancestor of Cass's."

"Correct. You see, sometimes people seem to possess amazing power when faced with impossible odds. That's because that's exactly what it is. In some people, even without being unmade, like your sister, their power leaks. I can only imagine how strong he would have been had he unlocked his true potential."

"Did her parents know? Her mom is Italian, right? Is that why they named Cassandra after him?"

"No. I think that is just a happy coincidence."

"Crazy. What about Jayce and Atara? Are they products of famous bloodlines too?"

"Well, I can't tell you much about Atara because there are some things that she has yet to learn and accept. As you know she was adopted and never knew her birth parents. She grew up loved, but she always felt different, like she wasn't as important since her parents didn't want her. Atara needs to realize just how special she is."

"She's a good person. I can tell."

"That she is. As for Jayce, one of his family members long ago had been unmade and one of his other family members had been a very successful soul tamer. In fact, she still is."

"So, does Jayce know that he has family here? Can they meet?" I ask, growing excited for my friend.

"He has been made aware of his lineage, but at this time, they are unable to meet."

"That sucks. At least he knows now. Hey, one more question."

"What is it?"

"Are you and I still going to train?" I ask with a smirk.

Dorian bows with another smile. "I thought you'd never ask."

Chapter Thirteen

*W*ind whips around Dorian, blowing his gray tunic back and forth. Its violent blowing is in opposition to his calm demeanor. I watch him closely and try to stand my ground as the wind tries to cut into me. He picks up his power one last time in demonstration before snuffing it out completely. The dust settles back to the earth, but it looks like a tornado touched down.

"Your weapon doesn't determine whether you can use your chosen element. It can enhance it, complement it, but that elemental power is already inside of you. In your case, you have versatile weapons, but those fans will work best if you're using wind power every time. Because of that, you need to learn to hold onto that element at all times."

"How hard will that be?"

"For anyone but you or I, incredibly difficult. Now, let's begin."

I remember how it felt when I was angry with him and Micah. The power came so easily then. It's a bit more difficult now, but I still manage.

"Good. Now, imagine you have a dial and keep the setting on low. Now, we're going to spar and you're going to keep that wind power in check at that level."

"Okay, I'll try." I get into a fighting stance and wait for Dorian to go on the offensive, but he motions me forward. I oblige.

It's even harder than I thought, splitting my focus like this. Holding onto my power is like trying to grip a stick of butter in a pot of oil. Keeping both powers separate has proven to take all my focus. In turn, my attacks are weaker. Dorian makes me pay for that.

He doesn't fight meekly; everything is so dominant and controlled. When he punches, the air slams into me like a bullet. When he kicks, he cuts through the air with no resistance. Everything is a brutal grace. He manipulates everything to his advantage. He makes me feel it all.

He's not even using a weapon and is still able to keep me at bay. I try to press my luck when I see an opening, but with just a bit of wind manipulation, he turns me completely around and I spin right back around to try to attack. I flash in and out of existence in an attempt to gain the upper hand. I try to catch him from the side with a high kick. He ducks under it too quickly. I get frustrated and he goads me into making the move that he wants. I end up on my back.

"Wind has many advantages, Jasmine. You can feel your opponent's moves before they reach you or just the slightest manipulation of it can throw your enemies off balance or you can redirect their attacks. It's all up to you and how quickly you can react." He continues to coach me as he attacks.

Dorian barely gives me time to react. It makes me careless and he knows it. But, he also knows that I can figure out what I'm doing wrong by watching him. Dorian wants me fighting on instinct. He wants me to be like the wind and be able to change direction or tactics smoothly.

I follow his dance and still successfully keep my power in check after a while. We train for six hours, taking three breaks in between. When we finish, I feel like I have no energy left inside me. This has been the most intense training yet.

Dorian had me incorporate all the elements of our training thus far, and he made me go at full speed as much as I could manage. We did a bit of traveling, fighting with our weapons, even teaching me a bit about my seals, hand to hand, weapon against hand, vice versa, and even fighting with my eyes closed. I had to trust myself to feel his spirit energy and to listen to what my body was telling me. I did all of this while trying to keep my wind power in check and at the ready.

On the final leg of our training, Dorian had me unleash all the power I could manage, trying to attack him at different distances. Then, I worked on more controlled wind attacks, struggling to land attacks with precision. He'd assured me that I'd get it and that I was doing an excellent job I have no choice but to trust his word.

"We'll be doing more of this soon, but I believe that Gwyn has the pleasure of working with you next. Just be aware that she's a hard ass."

"Even more than you?" I ask jokingly.

"Much more than me. Be very afraid," he chuckles. "Now, go home and meditate. You need to talk to your friends tomorrow."

"Alright. I'll be ready."

"Good, and Jasmine... you should be holding onto your power." He disappears leaving me to journey home alone.

I almost go back, but that vision once again immobilizes stops me. Blood, screams, destruction- it all flashes in front of my eyes. It can be prevented. I conjure my weapons. I don't need a break. I need to make up for the time that I locked myself in my room.

Hector, I hope that I can live up to the legacy that you left.

I hope that I can keep my people alive.

◊◊◊

"So, I'm sorry that I pushed you all away and hurt your feelings, but I was afraid for my sister and I wanted to punish them. I felt used and I felt that it was their fault. I didn't know how to deal with it and I definitely didn't want to talk about it with you," I tell the trio. Each of them have different expressions, ranging from hurt and disappointment to understanding. Getting the story from me has opened up more questions.

They ask me what I know about the Immortals and being unmade. I give them a brief rundown and Atara tells me she thinks it's cool that my sister and I are fighting for the same thing. Then, it's time to tell them what Dorian told me about my family's background.

"There's one more thing that I wanted to say. It's only right that I tell you since Dorian told me about you guys, well, except for you, Atara."

Atara frowns, but it disappears quickly. Perhaps, she already knows whatever it is or maybe they're still searching for answers for her.

"Unless they already told you why I'm so important."

"No, they didn't," Jayce says with a bit of harshness in his voice.

I didn't mean to upset him, but clearly, he's not over it. We'll have to talk about it when this is over.

"Okay, well, there was a guy named Hector. He was what they call a transcendent or abyss walker. He was the son of a human woman and a Soul King. He's my ancestor and apparently, the power he had still runs pure inside of me." I try to make it seem as if it's no big deal. I mean, it's not like I've had this power available to me the entire time.

"So... you're part angel? No wonder everyone thinks you're so cute and innocent," Cass says, slowly processing it.

I hold up my thumb and pointer finger. "Well, a very small part."

"Hell of a legacy," she compliments.

"Well, I can say the same for all of us," I respond, risking a glance at Atara. She has her head down in thought.

"Anyway, there's something about me being the last child of the Soul King that makes me have even more responsibility. It's some prophecy that they made. I don't even know what happened to all of the other descendants." I don't tell them about my vision. My instincts tell me to keep it to myself.

"Thank you for letting us know, Jazzy. I hope that you can come to one of us if you need to talk about things that are bothering you," Atara says.

"Or, at least deal with it on your own and not bail on us. There are some things that we can't do without the whole team," Cass says without any hint of anger.

"You're right. It's not just about me. I will work twice as hard when we train so that I won't let you down."

Jayce turns away as if he doesn't believe me.

"Jayce," I say loudly to get his attention. He looks up slowly. "I really am sorry that I hurt your feelings. I don't want you to keep your distance," I admit.

He stares at me for a few seconds, but then turns up the wattage on his smile. "I suppose that I can look past it this one time."

"Thank you. That means a lot." I smile back and Cass rolls her eyes.

"Look, I think we're making Cassie uncomfortable," Jayce jokes as he notices the same thing. He casually wraps an arm around her shoulder and pulls her in close. "Really, Jazzy is like the little sister I never had."

"If you say so," Cass responds as she ducks under his arm. "You guys are just too sensitive for me. You're both like little girls."

"Or, we're like young adults that aren't afraid to express our feelings," I defend.

"Yeah, even though you're dead doesn't mean you don't have a heart, geeze," Jayce says.

Cass and Jayce continue to bicker back and forth while Atara opens and closes her mouth like a fish. It's obvious that she wants to say something, but with motor mouth and grumpy gills, it's kind of hard. So, I clear my throat loudly. They stop long enough for me to give Atara a look to tell her that that's her cue to speak.

"Uh, I kinda know what happened to me. Why I was adopted. I didn't want to say anything, but I feel like I should." Her voice is even quieter than usual. It's bothering her.

"I was thinking that we have a descendant of a warrior, someone whose family line is full of heroes, a person with the blood of an angel flowing through her and then there's just me."

"Not just you, Atara. You're-,"

"Hey, you don t have to make me feel any kind of way. When you're adopted, sometimes you just always feel different, even when they do everything to not make you feel that way. I guess I had a different reason for feeling the way I felt." She smiles at each of us and even though there's relief in her eyes, there's also a hint of sadness that will probably never leave.

"Gwyn told me that my parents wanted me, so that's good news." She smiles again before taking a deep breath. "My dad and mom were separating however, because my mom fell in love with someone else. He was a vampire, but my mom didn't know that at first. Right after I was born, my dad died from heart problems he had ever since he was little. By this time, the vampire had already told my mom the truth and when my dad died, she freaked out and asked for the vampire to turn her."

We're all leaning forward, listening intently to the story. Atara's hands begin to shake. Cass notices it too and she narrows her eyes.

"You don't have to tell us if it makes you uncomfortable," Cass assures her.

"No, it's not that I'm uncomfortable, it's just like I'm now in mourning about something else, ya know?"

"Yeah, I get it. I just don't want you to feel obligated," Cass says.

"Thanks. I'm okay. Really. So, my mom wanted to be a vampire. I don't know if he agreed or not, but he had some enemies that made sure it would never happen. I don't know the full story with that- she couldn't tell me. But, his enemies punished him by killing my mom. So, both of my parents were dead, just like that and I was a little baby."

"Atara, that is so terrible. I'm really sorry to hear that," I say.

She nods her acknowledgement. "Well, the vampire took me all the way across the country and called in favors to make sure I found a good home. He checked on me a couple times, I guess. Then, his enemies caught up with him and killed him too."

She takes a deep breath and continues. "When I was about five, I got really angry with a kid on the playground. After that, all the kids around me began to scream that they were burned. A few days later, some woman came to talk to my mom. I never got angry like that again and I didn't remember that until Gwyn brought it up to me."

"What was it?"

"Apparently, they sent a soul tamer down to seal my powers because I was so strong. I had the ability to manipulate fire when I was only five years old. But, it's just ridiculous that the power inside me is what killed me. If it wasn't sealed, the fire would have never harmed me." Atara unleashes a flame and it spreads from her palm to her shoulder without burning her.

The heat is intense, yet she stands before us as if nothing's wrong.

"I think that's why I'm so calm now. Fire can easily get out of control if you're not careful. It needs someone strong-willed to tame it. At least, that's what Gwyn said." She puts the fire out with a clench of her fist.

Someone's been practicing.

"So, you were so bad ass that you had to have a soul tamer come and seal your power. You do know that's amazing, right," Jayce says with a smile.

"He's right. I'm sorry that I ever thought you were weak," Cass says.

"It's okay. Natural talent doesn't equate to skill if I don't learn to use it. That goes for you too, Jasmine," Atara says.

"I hear you. I don't even know what powers I really have yet," I tell them as I still hold onto my wind magic. It's so faint that they don't even notice it. But, boy if it isn't draining.

"We all have a lot to live up to. But, let's surpass all the expectations. I want to be the best. And, I want a nickname," Jayce says with a straight face.

"Then, maybe we should stop talking and get to work," Cass suggests.

I think of all the training I had just done and open my mouth to say, "Tomorrow," but the vision flashes in my head once more and I look at all my friends that are counting on me...

"Only if you can keep up."

Chapter Fourteen

*M*onths pass as we train like crazy. Each of us have been getting better by miles. Because of this, we've been going on team hunts. There's been three this week. Escorting a soul, tracking a dark spirit, and sealing an escaped soul. In a few hours, we'd be going on another. I've decided to paint while I wait until it's time to rendezvous with the others.

I've been working on painting my fans. I've left one fan open and one closed lying beside it. Bringing out the details and beauty of my weapon has made me feel more connected to it. After all, they are part of me. Soon, I'm consumed in the reds, whites, and silvers that I'm using and don't even realize that time has gotten away from me. Jayce brings me back to reality.

"Uh, hello there. Earth to Jasmine."

"Huh, oh. Hey. What time is it?" I ask as I place my brush down.

He assesses my painting with his head tilted to the side. His blue eyes look darker as he studies my work. "It's that time, girly. And you're not ready."

I give him a once over. We'd all decided that when we go on these missions, we'd dress the part. Tonight is no exception. He's wearing a fitted sleeveless black shirt with silver patterns that look like lightning bolts all over it. His bottoms stop at his calves and are silver and black as well. On his left arm is a black wrap with a yellow symbol on it that's a gift from Kenji. He hasn't told me what it means yet.

Those beautiful blue eyes of his shine brightly with excitement. His curly black hair lies perfectly in place. That has to be one of his supernatural powers. Casanova.

"Give me a second." I close my eyes so that I can focus on the details of my outfit. They want me to be The Eternal Flower. I have to look the part. I'm wearing a white, shimmery, nearly see-through sleeveless jacket that hangs mid-thigh. Underneath, I have on a red shirt that crisscrosses in the front, showing just a tiny bit of my stomach and stops at my hips. Then, I'm sporting black shorts and white slip on shoes that also have the same otherworldly shine as crushed jewels as my jacket. I got the idea from looking at all the architecture around me.

Jayce silently judges my outfit. "How do you get that translucent, ethereal look with the jacket?"

"Magic." I wink and disappear.

I hear him groan as he follows closely behind. I appear at the meditation area where Atara and Cass are patiently waiting. Neither one comments on my tardiness.

Atara seems to have just as much fun in creating her image as I do. She has on purple, fingerless, fishnet gloves that wrap around her middle finger and stop at her forearms. She's also wearing a black half-shirt that has a fishnet design in the back and a purple mask that covers her nose and mouth. She looks like a ninja that loves fashion. Her hair is tied up high, exposing her nape undercut. She's also wearing form-fitting leather pants sit low on her hips. Even I must admit how beautiful she looks.

Cass is dressed much more simply and it suits her. Her hair is pulled back and braided. She has on a baby blue and black compression one piece that has crisscross buttons in the front until it reaches the middle of her chest. The top has slits on the sides in the shape of a "v" that expose the side of her toned stomach. Then, the shorts stop mid-thigh, hugging those muscles snugly. She's also wearing leather gloves with the fingers out.

Cass really was meant for this. This is the most beautiful I've ever seen. Her aura is humming. She's ready.

"Now that we're all here, let's go over the plan. Atara and Jasmine are going to draw them in by using their attacks. If Jayce and I can land fatal blows, so be it. If not, we'll try to hold them enough for you two to seal them." Cassandra has been coming up with the plans and has become our de facto leader. No one has questioned it yet.

"And, if there's more than two, we split up. Jayce and Jasmine, Atara with me. That way our skills will be evenly distributed. And let's do this quickly. I don't want to hear any of their mouths."

"Sounds good." I up the power of my wind. I've been doing that little by little each day in order to expand the amount that I can hold onto. It's still exhausting, like sprinting everywhere all the time, but I'm getting better.

"They're waiting for us," Jayce says. A second later, I feel Micah's energy like a soft touch on my hand. "Let's go."

Jayce takes the lead and we head to our new battleground. This world is rugged, full of cliffs, trees, hills, and choppy water below. We are standing on a cliff that's overlooking a waterfall. On the other side of the water is a dense forest area. Even from this distance, I can feel malevolent energy and plenty of it. It's stronger than we've ever fought before.

Atara and Jayce share a look and Cass just squints as if she can see through the thicket of trees. Maybe she can. It really wouldn't surprise me. At least they all seem to know that this isn't going to be as simple as we thought.

"I'm going to assume that you all feel them inside there. That's good. This forest is a hub for dark energy. Every time we exterminate the beings inside of there, we always have to do it again every few months or so," Kenji tells us.

"We don't know why they gather, but we do know that too much of them in one place is never good. That's where you come in. I feel about fifteen, no twenty low level demons. Do take care of them," Gwyn says.

"Twenty? Anything else we should know about them?" I ask, trying to ignore the sinking feeling in my stomach.

"That's for you to figure out. You're all smart," Dorian responds.

"But, I'll give you some advice. Watch each other's backs. Come find us when you're finished," Micah says.

"Wait? You're not staying to guide us? Aren't you soul guides?" Jayce asks rapidly.

"This is us believing in you. Don't let us down," Kenji says.

"If we feel that you're truly in danger, we will come. We're connected, remember?" Micah smiles at me before they all disappear, leaving us alone.

We all spread out amongst the cliffs so that we can get a better view of our enemies in the forest. We all try to feel for them. I take a deep breath and try to pinpoint twenty different energies. It's extremely difficult to hold onto all of them.

"I've found them all," Cassandra says with a quiet resolve.

I breathe again, pushing out my power so that the wind can help me. It makes it easier and I lock onto their locations.

"I feel them too," Jayce says. Atara and I nod.

"Good. Jasmine, you are going to take the left side of the river. There are three on the right that we'll handle. Since we have the element of surprise, we can take all four out alone and quickly. If we move fast enough, Jasmine, should be able to take out the second one, one hundred yards away on the same side. Us three will surround the cluster of three directly across from the one Jasmine will attack. By that time, she should be joining us as backup," Cass says.

"They'll know we're here by then," Atara points out.

"I'm sure they will. That's why we need to strike fatal blows swiftly. Don't push your power until we're right on them. There will only be two left on the right. Atara and I will take down the furthest one while you and Jayce get the one at three o'clock. They'll all swarm by then. Jasmine, use your wind to push them back enough for Atara to get off a couple shots. Jayce and I will keep them busy while you two either seal them or keep them off balance with long distance attacks."

"Let's try to keep the fighting near that clearing," Atara suggests, pointing at an opening on the left side of the river.

"What do you think they're doing here?" I ask. Even our guides claim that they don't know.

"Now isn't the time to ask. Are we clear on the plan?" Cass asks.

I close my eyes and an image of me being dragged across the floor by the demon flashes before my eyes. Part of me wants to freeze up and curl into a ball, to hide and shrink into a dark spot where I'll be safe. I shake it away. "Let's end this," I say with resolve.

"Go!"

"We all disappear with supernatural swiftness. I appear about a foot in front of the first demon. It's a medium to low level one. Its head is shaped like a human's, but it's slightly abnormal and deformed. Its jaw is unhinged and full of hundreds of shark-like teeth. Its hands are long, clawed, and curved, unable to close completely due to how freakishly large the claws are. It has a long reptilian scaled tail that breaks off into three parts and its legs are the size of small tree trunks and covered in spikes. I don't want them stabbing me.

I have about a half a second quicker reaction than the demon. With the help of the wind and my fans, I swing with both arms extended and sideways to slice the demon's head off. The demon disappears in a burst of black smoke and sulfur. The other demons seem to react just as my comrades finish their foes. Their energy spikes as they turn their attention to where their kin's life force has been snuffed out.

I flash forward and appear directly above the next one. It looks up with round charcoal eyes just as I slam it into the ground with a blast of wind. It bounces back up like a ball. I rip a seal symbol from my ribbon and press it into the demon's forehead and roll away.

The demon roars as it disappears into a cloud of black dust. Through the trees, I whip around to find one of the demons trying to get away by leaping over Cass.

"No you don't," I growl as I swing two more blasts of air in the demon's direction. It hits him head on and Cass manages to stab it with her sais as the beast flies back toward her.

She gives me a nod of thanks and then she and Atara disappear. I flash to Jayce's side and together we go after the next opponent. I can feel the other demons making their moves as the rest realize that the others have been quickly defeated.

When we appear before the monster, I draw its attention, fans out and arms spread. I pick up speed and breeze right past it until I'm about ten feet behind the demon. It tries to turn to see both of us, its tail whipping back and forth. Jayce stands off to its left side, spinning his staff, looking for an opening.

I disappear again flinging wind from the right, above, and in front of the opponent in quick succession. It dodges all three attacks, but it loses sight of Jayce. He rams his staff into the demon's throat and follows up with a blow to its temple. As the demon stumbles, it lashes out with its signature razor sharp claws. Jayce parries, grabs it by its forearm and spins it into me. I follow up with a seal and it disappears into a dark haze of smoke.

Cass and Atara's energy washes over me and a second later, they appear behind us.

"It's not going to be that easy now. They're all coming at once," I tell them.

"That's okay. Let's go say hello," Jayce says.

"Try to keep them in front of you."

Cass takes off running before disappearing and reappearing on the other side of the river.

We do the same, weapons out. Atara pulls two arrows and releases them in quick succession. They impale two demons and then catch fire. I add some wind to feed the flames and the demons scream as the flame consumes them.

Eight left.

We reach the clearing and they burst through at the same time. Atara pulls another arrow. Jayce holds his staff in his right hand. Cass goes straight ahead. I go left and Jayce goes right. Atara holds her ground and begins shooting. I keep them at bay by blowing them to the center.

But, one is much faster than the others and dodges all my attacks. He tackles me and his leg spikes dig into my flesh causing me to scream in pain and surprise. We tumble on the ground and then I disappear, taking him with me. I drop him from about thirty feet in the air, disappearing again, landing on one knee.

My body heals slowly and I take a second to catch my breath as the demon hits the ground and slowly gets up. Another one appears directly behind me. I pull a seal from my ribbons. Then, I wait to put my plan in motion.

It doesn't take long for the first demon to stand completely. It leans forward and lets out an ear-piercing scream. Someone's mad. Well, it's going to get a lot worse. The demon shoots all the spikes from its legs at me, catching me off guard. Startled, I nearly stumble backward. By the time I regain my balance, two of the spikes pierce me in the leg and side. The pain forces me to drop my seal and one of my fans. My tools disappear back into the energy that created it.

"Jasmine!" Jayce yells from about fifty feet away. He tries to run to me, but is confronted by his own enemy.

I pull the spike out of my stomach with a scream and hurl it at the monster barreling toward me. It dodges, but it gives me an opening. Pulling the other spike, I disappear behind the demon and slam its own weapon in the back of its neck while he's still dodging. He drops and I leap over his body and face the last opponent.

With a smirk, I cross my arms and stare my opponent down. Adrenaline makes it easy to ignore the burning ache racking my side as my body slowly knits back together. Confused, the demon stops in its tracks. A second later, Cass appears in front of it, crouched low and cuts deep with both of her weapons. Jayce then finishes it off with a terrifying crack of its skull that has the demon disappearing like dust particles in the wind.

I look around and all the demons are eliminated. I can't even sense any dark energy. Good. Atara rushes over to check on me.

"Are you okay?" she asks as she assesses my injuries.

"Yeah, I'm good. It only hurts a little," I say with a smile.

"They really were going after you. I was scared for a minute there. They even sliced my shirt and my chest. I had to conjure a new one," Jayce whines.

"Poor shirt. We should have a funeral for it."

"Sarcasm isn't needed, Sandy."

"I said never to call me that," she says, voice rivaling an iceberg.

"My bad; I forgot." He smirks.

Atara rolls her eyes. Let's just get out of here."

"Sounds good."

We all make a move to travel back home, but nothing happens. We stare at each other in confusion before trying again.

Still, nothing happens.

And again...

"O-kay. Maybe there's a part two of this test that we don't know about," Cass offers.

"Well, let's look around," I say.

We split up and search for about five minutes, coming up with nothing. All of us meet back up at the clearing.

"This is getting old. Maybe the test is timed and we just beat the bad guys quicker than expected," Jayce says.

"This isn't a video game, Jayce," Cass snaps.

"Man, chill out. It was a valid idea," he argues.

"Whatever."

"I'm going to try to contact Micah," I tell them.

You're all finished. Come on back and we'll celebrate, he tells me.

That's the thing. We're trying, but we can't travel. We thought that you guys were still testing us.

What do you mean you can't travel?

We can't leave, Micah. We tried. I begin to panic. If he doesn't know what I'm talking about, then something's wrong. The connection disappears and I turn to my friends with panic filled eyes.

"What did he say?" Atara asks.

I open my mouth to answer, but Micah's energy appears from across the river. He's joined by our other guides. Gwyn tries to come closer, but she's rejected by some invisible barrier.

"What's happening?" Jayce calls as we run closer.

"We don't know! But, we're going to get you guys out!" Kenji yells as he tries to flood the barrier with energy. It crackles and sparks, but remains intact.

Dorian pulls his weapon and grabs onto his wind power. I feel his strength even through the barrier, my hair rising from static. Yet, even with his help, it barely even cracks.

"We need to help them," Atara says.

Before we make it to the barrier, a person appears before us. His shirt is off and he's covered from the neck down in intricate tattoos. His lower body is covered in black and gold metal armor. He has a gladius sword attached to his waist. The black metal seems to absorb the light around it like a black hole.

His eyes are an intense red and slit like a cat's. They're eyes of a predator, hungry, waiting for a chance to devour his prey. His hair is black as a raven. It's thick and messy looking as if he just got out of bed after a full night of tossing and turning.

I shiver as dark energy bathes me. It creeps up from my toes and tries to drown me in its power. I tell myself that I'm not truly suffocating. After all, I'm already dead.

He stands about ten feet in front of us and about fifteen feet from the barrier since he's actually standing on the water of the river. We all freeze as we look at this being in front of us. I try to remember what Micah told me about demons.

He disappears and stands less than two feet in front of Cass.

"Hello," he says in a sweet, calm, thickly accented voice that I've never heard before. Then, he punches Cass with a blast of power that sends her flying like a bullet. She slams into one tree, splitting it from the force. It begins to topple over as she still rockets through the air, crashing into another tree and finally lays lifeless on the ground.

"Cass!" Atara screams.

I whip my head back to the demon before us. He wipes his chest casually and smiles at us. I turn to find our guides eyes filled with complete panic. They turn up the juice on their power.

Atara runs to where Cass is lying and I attempt to put myself between the demon and them. Not that I could do anything about it anyway, but maybe I can keep his attention. He watches me carefully. It seems as if he's peering into my soul. My entire body trembles as my fight or flight instinct takes hold.

Jayce makes a move to attack, but I warn him off with a hand motion. The demon walks back across the water and turns to Jayce. His smile fades away.

"Listen to the girl, boy. Make no mistake. I will kill you."

"Jayce, Jasmine, get away from him!" Kenji cries.

Not sure where we can really run, we still defer to our guides. We both make a move to flee, but he reforms behind Jayce and touches two fingers to the back of his neck, stopping his energy flow like a faucet being turned off. Jayce falls to his knees and then to his stomach, out cold. I cry out in disbelief.

What is this? Why is he so powerful? We've been training this hard and for what?

"At least let me thank you," he says with a smile that says he knows something I don't.

"For what?" I ask quietly.

Our guides are still pounding away at the barrier and a few more tamers that I've never seen have joined them. I have to buy some time.

"For all the sacrifices, of course. I've been sealed here for so long, I think that I've been forgotten. So, I started calling for these demons to come, knowing such a high level of demonic activity would be cause for them to be extinguished. These sacrifices have allowed me to soak up every ounce of their power, to finally break free, and to make this powerful barrier that they're trying to break. A lot of my 'friends' died for it."

I can't believe it. We freed this monster and now we're all going to die.

"Who are you?" I ask.

"Ah, ah, ah, that's for you to figure out. Now, what to do until I regain all my strength."

Atara walks through the clearing holding onto Cass's limp form. I look down and Jayce is still out too. We're next. She sets Cass down gently and then conjures her bow and arrow.

"Atara, no," I say, but she ignores me. Her power sends chills through me like a bath of ice, but the power is all heat too. Cold rage.

The demon raises an eyebrow as she shoots three arrows in quick succession. With an outstretched hand, he stops the arrow's progress in midair. But, Atara's not done and with a word, the arrows explode into balls of flame.

He jumps back in surprise as the flames lick his hand. She shoots two more arrows, but he evades skillfully. Enraged, Atara runs straight at him and attacks.

She punches, he leans back. She punches again, he smacks her hand out the way. He ducks a high kick and then rolls out of the way of a follow up. The process repeats with him dodging and blocking every move. His eyes burn an even brighter red in excitement.

He's just toying with her.

But, fueled by her rage, Atara fights fiercely and quickly. Some moves I can barely keep up with. I want to help, but my feet won't move. My hands continue to shake.

He can destroy us all if he wants to.

I look back again and see that the barrier seems to be weakening.

There's a loud smack of flesh hitting flesh and Atara skids along the dirt about fifteen feet. But, she pops back up and goes after him again. She's relentless. He begins to laugh as he finally fights back getting faster and stronger every ten seconds. At this rate, it's going to be bad.

Flames skirt across her skin causing her body to glow as she dives out of the way of a leg drop that causes the ground to shake. She quickly changes directions and lashes out with a fiery fist. Surprisingly, it connects. His head snaps back from the blow, but he just chuckles. The flames burn out before they can do anymore damage.

"Jasmine," Jayce whispers as he tries to move. He's barely able to lift his head.

"Jayce," I say, sliding next to him on my knees. "They're going to help us in a minute. It's going to be okay."

"Help... her," he rasps.

"I-I can't. He's too strong."

"Please. Don't let her fight alone." He still tries to move. If he can stand, he'll force himself to join the fight. I can't let that happen.

I look at the guides once more. They're exhausted. Plus, there's no telling if they'll be able to travel once they get inside either.

Atara is starting to slow. Her movements begin to hesitate. She'll die for sure if I don't help her. The demon is putting a beating on her now. He punches her midsection and then flashes behind her and lands kicks to her back. Atara stumbles forward and ignites her hands to use the flames against him. But, he sends a roundhouse kick to her temple and she drops. Miraculously, she rolls on her side and pops back up. But, he's ready for her. I feel him call for more strength as he prepares for a finishing blow.

She won't be able to dodge, but I can help. My weapon's already in my hand. I deliver a swing that sends a gust of wind right into Atara. The demon puts too much into his swing and slides forward, too off balance to halt his attack. I pull two seals and then throw them at the demon, hoping to stun and then bind him. They make contact, but he only stiffens for a second and then turns to me with a growl.

Now, his eyes are completely black and I can see his dark aura surrounding him like an extra shadow hugging him. Instinctively, I take a step back. Out of the corner of my eye, I can see Atara pull another arrow.

"I will not be bound again." His voice is booming cannon- full of malice and the promise of destruction.

We stare each other down and I grip my weapons so tightly against me that they nearly crack. I imagine that I feel my heart beating one hundred miles per hour in my chest. I feel his energy shift before I feel him move. It rises inside of him like a tsunami and I'm too slow. He grips my arms to keep me from using my weapons and then floods me with his own power. The violence of his power rolls over me, beats at me, and pulls me under his murky depths.

Then, it happens again. The vision from before sparks inside my conscious like an ember growing into a great blaze. Fire, rage, screams. Bones are crushed, souls enslaved, worlds toppled. I feel it all. The pain of my comrades, the deaths that I couldn't stop, the destruction of everything that is beautiful and good. It hurts like nothing I've ever felt before.

I can do nothing but scream. His cries mirror my own. My brain shatters into a million pieces.

Wind spins around me like a tornado. Trees are uprooted. The earth moves. But, it hurts so bad that I can't do anything to stop it, even if I'm the one causing this.

He can no longer hold on.

The vision begins to repeat and speed up again as if trying to tell me to hurry and remember what's at stake. But, it hurts even more. The feeling of realness is overwhelming. Hands on my head, I fall to my knees.

I feel it all.

I feel everything.

Their pain, fear, deaths, suffering.

So much torment.

I am forever burdened with their struggles. There's a piece of myself that I think is lost forever. My heart feels like an open wound.

"Jasmine!" someone calls. "Stop!"

Everyone is blown away from me.

Finally, mercifully, the vision stops and I'm kneeling before the demon who clawed his way back to me if the marks on the ground are any indication. His skin is covered in tiny cuts and pieces of torn skin that are healing slowly.

"Your essence feels... familiar," he says to me.

"I can't let you live," I say back with much more certainty than I feel. I know however that it's very true. I stand slowly. The pain is still there gnawing at the back of my mind.

"As if you have the power or the will to stop me." His skin is once again flawless. He stands before me, arms crossed, daring me to make a move. His scowl is filled with hatred. It's almost personal.

I feel the barrier break, helped along by my own power. "Maybe not alone, but you see, my friends are all here."

Jayce has made it to his knees and Cass begins to stir as one of the soul tamers begins to heal her. Atara is limping, but she makes her way to me. She puts a hand on my shoulder. The demon growls as we all pull our weapons. The other tamers flank us.

"Even you know better than to take us all on," Atara says.

"Yeah, we're just getting started," Jayce says from behind me "I'd like to see you try that little trick on me again." His voice is low, deadly. His body language says that he's ready to draw blood.

We can travel now. I can feel it. That levels the playing field a bit.

"Well." He looks around. "As much as I'd like a taste of that mysterious energy of yours, it'll have to wait."

Something new flashes behind his eyes. It looks like fear, but the fear isn't because of us. He looks down at his hands, horrified. It gives me an opening, or so I hope.

He disappears just as I leap for him. I land in the spot where he just stood. "No!" He can't get away. I take off after him.

Micah anticipates my move, but I slip under his arms as he tries to grab me. "Jasmine, no. It's too-,"

But, I'm already gone, searching for his powerful, demonic energy. I cut through three different worlds as I attempt to track him. He's fast, but I'm determined. I don't know what I'll do when I find him, but... I have to do something.

The fourth world has his taint all around. I lock onto his location and then make the jump. But, when I reform on this plane, I wish I hadn't.

The heat is unbearable.

Volcanic eruptions are constant in the distance. Ash covers the sky and the rest of the world seems to burn. Rivers of lava cut through the land. Waves of heat blur my vision and distort the landscape, but I still see everything. Everything smells burnt. The smell coats my tongue until the ash coats my throat. Then, there's the demons. They're everywhere, I take a step back from the cliff that I'm standing on. Rocks crumble below my feet. It's only when I take a step back that I notice him out the corner of my eye.

I turn quick and pull my weapon, but he doesn't move. He's hunched over, hands on his head, knees on the ground. He's rocking back and forth, paying me no mind, as he mutters unintelligible words to himself.

In the back of my mind, I'm aware of the other demons that have noticed my arrival.

This isn't a good idea.

Obviously.

He finally turns to me, eyes wild and red once again. All the courage I felt suddenly escapes me. He stands and looks at me with an expression of humanity. He even feels like an entirely new person.

"I remember now. I remember everything."

He takes a step toward me, hand outstretched.

I freeze under his gaze. I can smell the sweat coating his brow, the musty scent of being locked underground for so long. He's so close that he almost touches me, but suddenly, he jumps back as silver flames surround me. They shoot out in all directions, devouring dirt and the dust greedily. A second later, Micah's powerful body is covering mine and then we disappear.

He takes me to a room that I've never seen before. There are wide carpeted steps directly in front of me. They lead to a large seating area. The entire room is lit by long torches that cast the walls in shadows. The walls are held up by thick marble pillars. There's also a grand chandelier hanging from the high, patterned ceiling.

My quick once-over is finished. Everyone's here. He ignores them as he faces me, anger coloring every part of his face. There's a hint of disappointment mixed in there too. I have a hunch it's my fault.

"What were you thinking?" he roars. There are tiny flames still licking his skin. His power is a wild beast, scary, and unpredictable. I notice the toll that using it has taken on him even if his rage is masking it. "Do you want to die? Did you want your friends to die chasing you?"

I hang my head down in shame. "I'm sorry. I just felt like I had to. He's not supposed to get away." It sounds pitiful coming from my mouth.

"And then what? We don't even know who he is. He put up a barrier that we could barely penetrate and he dropped two of you with no effort. He toyed with Atara and at least she tried. If you wanted to do something, why didn't you help her sooner?" His voice is still raised, but those flames are finally dying down.

I look around at everyone. My team and our guides are here, but there are other soul tamers here as well. Six more of them. They are all assessing me as if thinking, 'so this is the child that's supposed to save us all. Ha. What a joke.' I raise my head defiantly.

"I'm sorry. That was directed toward Atara. I let you down again. It will not happen a third time." She nods. "I can't explain why I did it. It was stupid," I say to Micah.

"You're damn right it was. You will not do that again. If any of you see him again, you will run. Am I clear?" Micah asks with extra bass in his voice.

"Okay," I say.

Satisfied, he sighs and takes a step back. Then, he finds a wall to hold him up, his anger is the only thing keeping him upright.

Kenji takes the floor. "Angelina, Niko, and I will begin tracking him so that we may plan our next move."

Two other soul tamers step forward and bow. Niko seems to be about fourteen or fifteen and Angelina is probably about twenty-one. They must be trackers like Kenji.

"We were going to allow you four to go on runs together without our supervision, but that will have to wait until we access the threat. I'm sorry, but that will go for all new teams and individuals. There needs to be at least two guides along for now," Dorian orders.

"Understood," another female guide says.

Another one stares at Jayce before nodding. That must be Mateo. Short, toffee colored, clean cut facial hair, muscular, cute.

"Before we depart, I want to recognize Atara for her bravery in the face of danger. Without hesitation, she leaped into the fray to protect her friends and she did so with an incredible show of strength and will. We all felt that blast of cold, intense power. It settled into our bones as if the heat of it would freeze our very souls. Thus, you have earned your name. Your allies and enemies alike will know you as the Winter Dragon. May your reputation strike fear into the hearts of all those that oppose you." Gwyn smiles at her protégé.

Atara's eyes are wide with surprise, but she puts on a calm demeanor. "I am humbled. I hope that I can make you proud."

"You already have," Gwyn says.

"Congratulations, Atara," Micah says with a smile.

Well, at least he's happy with one of us. I steal a glance at Jayce and Cass. They both look as if they want to hide in a corner somewhere. Cass must hate that she never had the chance to prove herself. Jayce, there's no telling with Jayce.

Kenji must notice it too.

"You two have absolutely nothing to be ashamed of. You completed the task you set out to do and you excelled. Hold your head high. Who's to say that any of us would have done better?"

Cass grits her teeth, but then finally says, "Okay," quietly.

But, she's anything but okay. And, she's not happy with me, either. Her death glare proves that.

"We need to go," Angelina says.

I stare at the new tamer. She's the most unique person that I've seen thus far. She's tall and curvy. Her skin is porcelain. Her head is completely shaved and tattooed the way people get henna on their hands. She has two different color eyes- one blue, one green.

"Okay. You finish things here. Us three will go and you four will start the patrols," Kenji says.

"Agreed."

With that, they disappear leaving us alone with Dorian, Gwyn, and Micah.

"We'll keep you all safe, don't worry. Nothing like this has ever happened," Dorian says.

"You have no idea who he is?" Cass asks. She's still in a lot of pain, but I don't think anyone notices but me. It's in the slight sag of her shoulders, her slow breathing, the way she grits her teeth.

"No, but we're conferring with the elders. They're like us, but far older. Probably the first soul tamers. They've seen it all. They've survived it all. The Soul Kings are remaining silent which only worries me more," Gwyn says.

"Great. Just great,'" Jayce mutters. He's scared. I don't blame him. I was too.

"It's not for you to worry about. The only thing you all need to focus on is getting stronger," Micah tells us.

"For now, you all need some rest. You'll have tomorrow off," Dorian says.

"I don't need rest; I need-," Cass begins.

"You need to rest. It's not up for debate, Cassandra," Dorian says in a low voice.

She looks utterly defeated. She reminds me of a deflated balloon. "I could have died," she says in a whisper.

"What?"

"I could have died because I wasn't prepared. He hit me once. One blow nearly ended me. I couldn't move, I couldn't dodge. I didn't even feel him come after me. None of us are strong enough," she growls. Her anger is tangible and suffocating.

"And you will be. But, you can't push yourself to these limits if you're not getting rest too. I know it was an eye-opening experience, but you lived to fight another day. Be proud of that," Gwyn says.

"Yeah, at least I had a good reason not to fight," she says, clearly directing that at me.

"They told us to run, Cass. It wasn't our fight. You didn't feel his energy the way I did. You didn't see what I saw. You have no idea, Cass," I defend.

"And when Atara didn't run, you should have stood beside her. You abandoned us twice now!"

My anger switches on like a light. I turn to hold her gaze, my hair whipping behind me. My power begs to be released, to be let free of its chains, to find a target for my growing rage. "You weren't even awake! You don't even know-,"

"Enough!" Atara cries. The cold heat of her power surges, slamming into my own and pushing it back.

Everyone is surprised by her sudden confidence. I take a step back so that her power can stop pushing against my own. They are not my enemies.

"Jasmine is right. What I did was stupid. I was blinded by my emotions and that's not how you win fights. I don't take what I did back though. If I hadn't done it, who knows what would have happened. His power was, wow. It was insane, but I didn't care. I'm part of a team too. It wasn't fair of me to force Jasmine into an impossible choice."

Now I'm taken aback.

"Don't make excuses for her." Cass is really trying to pick a fight with me.

"I'm not. I don't regret what I did, but I don't blame her. Besides, in the end, she's the crazy one that went after him alone. Why did you do that?"

Everyone turns to me expectantly.

I think about my vision and how I felt that he was connected to it. I'm still not ready to tell them. Dorian gives me a knowing look.

"I don't really know how to explain it. It just felt like something really bad would happen if I let him leave."

Jayce, who's been uncharacteristically quiet snorts. "Well, we all know how that turned out."

I roll my eyes. I'm tired of feeling like the bad guy. I don't have to explain myself to them. "Can we go now?"

Atara watches me very closely as if she knows I'm hiding something. I try to ignore her.

"Yes," Dorian says with a sigh. "I think that's more than enough for today. We'll escort you home and then there's no more traveling until we say."

"Okay," we all agree.

Cassandra heads to the lake to speed up her healing while the rest of us head to our respective quarters. I walk around pacing for a good ten minutes to make sense of my visions.

But, nothing becomes any clearer. There's only blood and death. I don't see the demon's face specifically as I search my memories. But, I still can't shake this gut feeling that he's connected in some way.

Not surprisingly, I feel Atara's energy forming inside my room after we've been back for about an hour. I continue to pace, but motion for her to have a seat. She watches me with her compassionate gray eyes, but I try to ignore it. I don't need a therapist right now.

Finally, she speaks up. "Something happened, didn't it?"

Yeah, our friends got their butts kicked."

"Jazzy, you know that's not what I mean.

I stop pacing and lie on the floor, arms and legs spread. It's not as comfortable as my bed, but it still feels like I'm lying on feathers. "I never asked to be special," I say so quietly that I don't think she heard me.

"You can tell me and if it's a secret, I'll keep it." Then, she gets up and lies next to me on the floor. She's turned on her side and her arm is supporting her head.

"I'm seeing things, Atara. Bad things. Like the world being torn apart and rebuilt in fire and brimstone. I don't know how else to explain it. It happened once and then again while you were fighting. It's like my vision was trying to tell me something about that demon. He's a part of it somehow. He could be the reason."

Atara just stares at me as if she doesn't believe me- no, she believes me, but she doesn't want to believe.

"They'll take care of it," she says with more confidence than her eyes show. The fear behind them mirror my own.

"Atara, I don't think they can," I reply softly.

"And you think you can?" It isn't mocking or an accusation.

"As I am now, I don't know, but why else would it be shown to me?"

"I don't know. What does it mean? Are we really ready for what's coming?"

"I don't know that either. But, I don't want the others to know yet. I don't want them to be afraid like I am."

"You're not a coward, Jasmine."

"I don't know what I am. But, I know what everyone expects me to be."

"You'll be all that and more."

"Only because I have no choice," I say with a snort.

"There's always a choice, even for us. Look, I know Jayce is like your bestie or whatever, but I like to think that I can give you different insight too. We're not so different, Jazzy." She gives me a soft smile.

She's right. On the outside, our similar skin tones, looks, and body types could make people think we're related. Even our temperaments and demeanors are similar. But, Atara's a better person than me. She just doesn't know it.

"Thanks. I just don't want to give this burden to anyone else yet. Not even you. But, I can't hide it forever."

"Just don't do anything stupid like try to go after him again. You're not ready. We're not ready."

I don't respond. Atara sits up and pulls me up with her.

"We'll train morning and night if we have to, but you're not going to go looking for him; do you hear me? They'll know anyway."

I nod.

"Why don't I believe you? Do I have to share a room with you so I can watch you?"

"No. I'm not going to just go after him again without being prepared."

"But you do want to go after him again?"

"I may not have a choice!"

"You keep saying that."

"Because sometimes it's true."

Chapter Fifteen

That night, I dream of the demon. He's following me everywhere I go, but doesn't make a move. I just sense his presence lurking in the shadows. Behind a tree, behind a building off in the distance. I turn, but I don't see him. Still, I know he's there. Every time I jump, every time I move to another plane, his red eyes are focused on me.

Finally, I grow tired of the game and seek him out. When he realizes that I'm coming toward him, he leaves his hiding space and calls my name. I take another step and he reaches for me again, red eyes flashing to black. His teeth are turned in a wolfish grin, ready to consume me. I know there's a promise of death in his embrace, but I still find my feet moving forward.

Before we close the distance, something wakes me. It's like a rope dragging me back to my world. I nearly curse as Jayce plops on the bed beside me. He is staring right at me, expression unreadable. His baby blue eyes are darker than usual, as if the color is connected to his mood.

"Well, good morning to you too," I grumble, kicking the blanket off my feet. The fogginess of my brain clears quickly. Being scared half to death will do that to you. Or, would it be half to life in my case?

"Come with me," he demands.

I frown. "Are you okay? We can't travel anywhere, remember."

"Sorry. I forgot. I just… need to talk to you."

I stand up and he follows. We face each other and I tilt my head to the side as I read his energy. It's suppressed. It doesn't feel completely like Jayce. The dark eyes, my dream, his forceful demands. It all feels so wrong. I take a step back, ready to disappear or at least contact Micah when he holds up a hand to stop me. I freeze.

"Wait, please," he begs, allowing Jayce's image to fall away. It's as if he's a snake shedding his skin. I'm too in awe of the trick to move.

In front of me now is a shirtless man covered from the neck down in tattoos, his skin a beautiful olive color. He's about 5'11". His eyes are red, but there's no weight of malice in them. His nose is narrow and slightly pointed. As I look at his face, I realize that he's not as old as he seemed before. He's probably about eighteen or nineteen.

His hair is groomed. It's still thick and full, combed back. He has long side burns and a hint of stubble around his goatee. The sword on his waist is nearly as long as his leg and his armor is shiny and black. The gold accents on it are symbols, much like the symbols on his tattoos. But, by glance, I can tell that they're different. I look back up to his lips. His top lip is thinner than his full, bottom lip and there's a small scar just above it. Overall, he has a very memorable face.

The fact that he's nothing at all like before seems to scare me even more. He could be unpredictable.

He runs a hand through his thick, black hair. It barely moves. "It is not my intention to hurt you." His remorse is painted all over his face, but that doesn't make it true.

"You tried to kill my people. You nearly did."

"I had lost myself then. There were other factors at play. I am in control now. I promise you."

I stare into his eyes, wary. I should just call Micah and all of this will be over. But, I can't. My gut tells me not to.

"Who are you?"

He bows, but never takes his eyes from me. "My name is Augustus, and I used to be a soul tamer like you."

I frown and take a step back again until I bump into the wall. "Now, you're lying. You're a demon," I accuse. The eyes, the energy. He's demon. There's no denying that.

"You're right. I do carry demon blood inside of me, but only because the Soul Kings demanded it."

"What? I-I don't understand." I look around, weighing my options. He'll never let me just leave. If he thinks I'm calling for help, he'll stop me. I lost my window with my stupidity I have no choice but to listen. If he wanted me dead, he could have killed me in my sleep. No, he wants to manipulate me.

"Oh, Princess there is so much that you don't know. I knew I felt something in you. I recognized your soul, your blood. You are Hector's. Your aura, it sings a familiar song."

My eyebrows touch the top of my forehead.

"Princess? I'm not a princess."

"Technically, no. But, you may be the closest thing to it in this world. I apologize if I've made you uncomfortable. Hector sent me to you."

"Hector is dead."

"I know. But, he was a friend and his spirit has spoken to me, brought me back from the brink of savagery. He helped me to remember the me that I once was. If you know of Hector, you know of the abyss walkers. But, do you know of the soul tamers that bound their flesh to demon's spirits so that they could be even more powerful?"

"No. They didn't tell me that." Because it didn't happen is what I want to say.

"That is because it was done in secret. Most of us became corrupt and had to be destroyed. I was losing myself as well, so Hector bound me as a final mercy. I started off forgetting who I was, who my friends were, that I was good, not evil, that I didn't get satisfaction from killing. He couldn't kill his only friend, he said. By that time, the demon inside of me had nearly taken over. I began to believe that I was a demon."

"Why would they do that? Isn't it cruel to leave you sealed for eternity? Why would he- I just don't understand."

"Desperation. He thought that he'd find a way to save me. Let me show you my story, and then you can decide for yourself."

"What do you mean?"

"I know you've been having visions. I had one too. You saw me. I remember that you followed me. I came to show you the truth. You must awaken your mind so that you can fight the darkness."

I hadn't even seen him move. He stands in front of me and pins me against the wall. Then, he places his thumb against my forehead and a bright light explodes in front of my eyes. I gasp at the pain and blink away the lights. When my eyes adjust, I am no longer standing in my room.

The world seems so bright- new. Empty. There are no cities, no roads, no cars in sight. Here, there's not much of anything. Yet, there's nothing peaceful about this emptiness. The air smells like death.

The scene changes abruptly. I am thrust upon a one-sided battle. No, not a battle- a massacre. Augustus and one other are the only two standing. His fear becomes my own as I watch him face down a winged demon. Its wings have claws on the end and its face is gray, yellow eyes too big for his head, hundreds of tiny teeth shining with blood. It screams and sounds just like the promise of death would. It freezes my blood.

There are body parts everywhere. Pieces of flesh, hair, and bodily fluids paint the brown and yellow grass inappropriate colors. The smell of death mixed with the humidity of the day is nearly too much. Augustus tries not to vomit, lest he look away from his attacker. He's only equipped with a sharpened rock and his chest, face, and hair is already coated with sticky, dark crimson blood.

The other man looks like he's going to collapse at any second. He must've gotten a second wind because he turns and runs away while the demon is focused on Augustus. He nearly stumbles, but regains his footing as he looks around. But, there's nowhere to hide. With a swoop of powerful wings, the demon takes to the skies. He lands in front of the man and quickly impales him, lifting him high in the air, letting his blood bathe his face.

Augustus screams out, "Father!" His father left him to die, but he doesn't do the same. With a war cry, he rushes at the demon with his crude weapon raised as if it's a sword instead of a single rock.

The monster seems unaffected by his human opponent.

With his free hand, the demon grabs him by the neck raising him in the air too. His father's blood coats him as well. Then, with a wing, he disembowels Augustus, ripping his intestines free of his body. He lets out a gurgle, eyes wide in disbelief before they begin to glaze over in death.

The demon drops both bodies and the second he does, I sense the aura of a warrior. He rips open the world and slices the demon in half with a swipe of his sword. In a smooth motion, he spins and sheaths his sword onto his back.

He looks around at the devastation and then falls to his knees. "I was too late. I didn't even save one." Finally, he stands for a minute, scans the landscape, and walks over to Augustus. After studying him for about ten seconds, he disappears again.

His features are burned into my mind. He's tall. Even by today's standards, 6'6" is very tall. Every part of his body is in perfect proportion to his height. He has broad shoulders, a muscular back, thick, powerful legs, sculpted arms and abs. He's wearing some sort of gray loincloth shorts with long fabric that hangs in the front and nothing else. His skin is sun kissed, but a tint that is not just from his tan, but the natural light golden that is all genetics. He has ash brown, collar length hair, a thick goatee, sculpted jaw, and hazel eyes. I look at him and I just know. That was Hector.

Before I can process that I just saw my ancestor, the scene changes again.

Augustus is on his hands and knees trying to vomit, but he's dead. Nothing comes out, but he continues to dry heave as his stomach muscles clench and unclench. There's a soul guide there with him, but he's not listening to his soothing words. A couple of seconds later, Hector appears.

"Here, let me. I have business with this one," he tells the guide in a calm, deep and commanding voice that also sounds a bit like music to my ears. A rumbling bass drum.

The guide hesitates, unsure of the protocol, but relents. He leaves the two alone. Hector walks over to where he's hyperventilating. He places a hand on Augustus's back.

"Peace, my friend. You are safe now." He lets his energy wash over him.

Augustus gasps and then freezes as if Hector's controlling him. After about ten seconds, he looks up into Hector's eyes. Hector helps him up.

"I died," he says quietly.

"You did. I am sorry. I was unable to prevent your death. But, there is hope. Death is not the end for you, young warrior. You have a guide that will teach you all you need to know about the next step of your journey. I want you to know that I killed the monster that caused your demise. It may have come too late, but you can rest easy knowing the beast will never harm anyone again. Now, let your guide help you and I will be there to check on you soon."

Hector steps away, but Augustus stops him with his hand on his arm. "Wh-who are you?"

"My name is Hector and I am an abyss walker."

Time speeds up again and the scene stops with Hector and Augustus sparring almost too quickly for me to keep up with. Both of them have smiles on their faces as they trade blows and swings of their weapons. Hector stops a kick with his hand and then throws him over his shoulder. He makes his blade disappear, tucks into a roll, and then regains his feet. Augustus calls his weapon and makes it disappear again in quick succession. They clash once more, ducking and blocking, striking and punching. Hector is coated in sweat by the time they finish. They clasp each other's forearms and then hug.

Shortly, a soul tamer appears. His dreadlocks fall well past his buttocks. His chocolate skin seems even darker against his royal blue cloak with his hood down. He completely ignores Hector after not even bothering to hide his disgust. Hector waves it off when Augustus frowns at him.

"I must go tend to my family."

Augustus nods. "Be careful, my friend."

Then, Hector disappears.

"Must you be so open with your malice, Altair?"

Augustus stops three feet in front of him. He raises his arms in exasperation. This isn't the first time they've had this conversation.

"He is an abomination."

"He is a friend."

Altair ignores him. "Your presence has been requested. Please follow me."

Again, time skips.

Augustus is in chains. His arms and legs are shackled to the floor, his body creating a giant "x." A couple of people are marking his body in those intricate tattoos that he's sporting now with tools that look like paintbrushes and switchblades. He hisses in pain, but doesn't protest. Once they finish, they bring in two demons. It takes four men to hold just one.

The demon thrashes against its captors to no avail. Without much fanfare, a fifth person slits the demon's throat. Immediately, the rest begin chanting. I watch as the demon's soul begins to flow over to Augustus like incense smoke. His entire body jerks like he's having a seizure. The chains tug against his body like they're going to rip his limbs free. His head tilts back and his mouth opens.

Then, he begins thrashing as the demon's soul enters his body. He spasms violently. The muscles in his arms strain from the motions. His shoulder is almost pulled out of socket. The soul is completely absorbed and then Augustus slumps over, still held by the chains. Sweat coats every inch of him.

They continue to chant and all his tattoos begin to glow an eerie yellowish-white. It's almost like they're sealing the soul to him, binding it through the tattoos. Once the glow goes out, the chanting stops.

"Augustus?" one of the soul tamers asks. He lowers his hood on his robe and steps closer. His long red hair falls in a straight line down his back. His hands twitch as if he's ready to call his weapon if need be.

His head is still slumped down. "Just... get it over with," he whispers.

The second demon begins to chuckle. Until then, he had been eerily still. He looks awfully close to human too. Human-like facial features and upper body and animal-like lower half. It looks like it could be an elk or deer. His hooves help him tower over his captors. This one is strong.

"I've been wanting a new host," he says, voice sounding like his throat's been in a wood chipper.

They ignore him and bring him closer. He doesn't fight; in fact, he waits patiently, watching Augustus as if he has a secret that he can't wait to share with him. They slit his throat and start the process over again. This time, Augustus screams the entire time. It's a blood curdling sound that echoes off the walls and sends goosebumps to the flesh. Even the ones chanting pause for a beat.

But, they pick up the words with more force, trying to drown out his screams with their melodic voices. Their singsong voices wrap around me. But, the screams continue to compete for attention. This one takes even longer and Augustus's throat becomes raw. Finally, he stops screaming and seems to pass out. No one moves for a minute. The other soul tamers breathe heavily from their own efforts.

Then, he begins to laugh. It begins as light chuckles, then transitions to an all-out booming laugh that sounds like thunder clapping. It frightens some of his comrades. They take a step back, drawing their weapons.

When the laughing stops, one soul tamer steps forward. She has lilac eyes that are impossibly real. Impossibly beautiful. She has a feather braided in one of her many intricate braids. Her skin is the color of cinnamon and all her features are delicate, regal even. She looks like a princess.

"How are you feeling, my friend?"

He looks up, eyes changing from brown, to red and cat-like, to black goat slitted. He flashes a near perfect smile. "I feel terrific."

◊◊◊

With a gasp, reality slams back into me. I fall into Augustus's arms. He helps me to my bed and then chants something. Immediately the wave of dizziness recedes. I stare up at him with new eyes.

"August... I mean Augustus, I-,"

He smiles. "August is just fine. I like it."

"Where's the rest? I need to know."

"I think that you've seen all that you can handle. You've seen that I'm telling the truth. You don't need to see my fall as well. I don't believe that I'm ready to share those dark memories."

"So, why are you doing this? Showing me this. Our soul guides will understand if you tell them what happened. Show them what you showed me."

His demeanor changes. "They won't. There was a kill order on me. Kill orders are absolute. It doesn't matter how much time has passed. I am too volatile to be allowed to exist. But, I need someone to know the truth, to keep my secret."

"Why me?"

"Because you are Hector's and you've been shown the future. You are awakening. What is your name?"

"J-Jasmine."

"Jasmine." He grabs my hand.

"That is a beautiful name. Listen, Jasmine. I am demon, but I am soul tamer as well. But, I have no allies. What I'm going to do next will probably end in my demise anyway. I need you to help me remember who I am and what I fight for. It may seem like I'm doing evil, but it'll all be for the greater good. The Soul Kings have given me another chance to control my destiny."

"What are you talking about?"

"I'm going to become more demon as each day passes. I'm going to live among them and obtain information about the rise in demonic activity. I know about it. I can feel it. I want to know who's responsible and what that will mean for our continued existence."

"Are you crazy?"

He laughs. "What do you think? You've seen what I've gone through. That evil is still inside of me. It helped me break free of my bonds, but it will not rule me. I want to still be of use. I am a soul tamer first. I will fight to protect humanity as long as I am able. I will do so by any means."

"How can I trust you? I don't even know you. You could be lying right now. The demon could be controlling you."

"It is a decision that you will have to make. Follow your instincts."

"And what if I say no?"

He contemplates my question. "Then, I will do it on my own. Your decision will not change mine, Jasmine."

"You have to understand, August, this is all too convenient. You nearly killed us all. Now, you're in front of me telling me and showing me all these unbelievable things with magic I've never seen a soul tamer use. There are others that could-,"

"They are not you," he says firmly. He closes his eyes and sighs. "I have stayed here too long. I will come again. If the other soul tamers hunt me, I will attack. The demons must trust me. I need you to trust me. My power may seem foreign, but I was taught by extraordinary masters, sons of angels as well as soul tamers that have been here for eons."

"Why? Why me?"

"You already know the answer to that. Even if you continue to deny it. When you accept it, I will be here. I will even train you. I will make you powerful beyond your wildest dreams."

He bows to me and then disappears leaving me in my room that suddenly seems too empty and far too cold.

August...

Chapter Sixteen

I'm a mess of emotions finger painted by a toddler. I don't know how long I sit there thinking about what I just learned, but my thoughts are interrupted when Atara comes to see me again. She's dressed in a light pink summer dress. It painfully reminds me of home. I used to throw on my summer dresses when we'd go to family dinners on warm evenings. Lightning bugs would dance in the sky and you could smell barbecue for miles. My mom and I would share a dessert, but Rayne and my dad would get their own. Then, an hour later, my dad would take us on a motorcycle ride or we'd go swimming with my mom at home.

I try to hide my frown as the memories eat away at my heart, but she catches it anyway.

"What's wrong? Are you just waking up?"

"No, no. I've been just thinking of home."

"Oh, what about? Maybe talking about it will help you feel better."

I push August out of my mind as Atara sits down. I imagine myself in some shorts and a black tank top and even with polished nails. I was never allowed to have anything too fancy. My mom wanted me to enjoy being thirteen, not look like a baby hooker. Her words.

"Just summer. Being with friends. Barbecues. Trips. I don't think I'll ever stop missing it."

"I know what you mean. I was going to get my learner's permit. I had plans for that." She sighs and flops onto my chaise.

"I bet. My dad used to let me drive around our neighborhood with him in the car, but I always imagined taking a drive down the highway on a motorcycle, feeling the wind in my hair."

"You've ridden on a motorcycle? It always seemed so scary to me."

"Yeah. My dad and sister both knew how, but I was only allowed to ride with my dad. He liked to go fast and would take me for rides on the highway. He never let me ride for a long time though because he said I'd get sore."

"You really did have a good life, Jazzy. Hey, I just realized something. All of us left people behind that we love, but only two of us lost our parents. What if the more tragic our story, the stronger we are?"

I snort and she shakes her head.

"I wasn't really serious."

"I know, but you're not really lightening the mood. You're supposed to be the positive one, Atara."

"Is that so? I'll try to remember that for next time. So, what are you, then?"

I tap my chin in thought and plop next to her. "I'm the prissy rich girl."

Atara pushes me over. "Whatever."

"Well, you tell me then,"

"You're just the really friendly one. I'm the shy one. Jayce is the flirt of course, and Cassie is the bitchy one."

"So, what you're saying is we have all the ingredients for a good reality show."

"Yep. Now we just need a cameraman."

"Gwyn could be the host, Kenji could produce it, and Micah and Dorian could be security since neither of them like wearing shirts because they're secretly obsessed with their muscles."

"But, they do provide a nice view for all of us."

We both laugh.

"I feel like I'm going to go crazy here if I don't find other forms of entertainment."

"We'll figure something out. Why don't we see what our other friends are doing?"

"Sure, though I'm not sure they really want to be around me."

"I think they're more afraid than they care to admit. They just don't know how to deal with it. And if they can't find him, I think I'm going to have some nightmares myself."

"His power was incredible," I admit. I think about how gentle he was just being with me. But what he did to my friends did happen. There's a monster sleeping inside of him. I can't forget that.

Something about him makes me want to forget.

"I can't believe we accidentally released him and I can't believe they have no idea who he is. We walked right into his trap like flies to fly paper. I mean, who sealed him then and why? Why don't they say anything? Even if that person is gone, someone else would have to know something, right?"

"I don't know. Maybe there's a place that we can look up things on our own. There has to be a hall of records or a library or something." I don't think that they would allow all this knowledge to just be passed on through word of mouth.

"You're right. It would be nice to know our history. Doesn't hurt to ask." Thinking about it now, maybe they should have been teaching us these things all along.

"So, what do you want to do first?" I ask, letting her take the lead.

"Let's go check on Cassie. She's going to give us the most trouble."

"Alright. Lead the way."

Atara gives a psychic knock on Cass's door and then a second later, she disappears. I join her. Cass is sitting on the floor leaning against the wall, knees to chest in some navy-blue sweats and a white t-shirt. Her hair is down and she looks like someone just told her that the monster underneath the bed just ate her puppy.

"Hey," I say gently when she doesn't look up.

"Hi," she responds quietly. She continues to stare straight ahead like a kid looking out the window on a rainy day.

"Do you want to talk about it?" Atara asks. She sits next to Cass and crosses her legs so that her dress isn't exposing anything. Very lady-like.

"It's just that everything feels so real now. My eyes are wide open. Everything just got put in perspective."

Failure will do that to you. It makes you humble yourself if you want to move forward.

"And we believe that you can lead us. Don't we, Jazzy?"

I smile at Cass as she finally looks up. "You're more than capable. I trust your judgment."

"I can't even unlock all my power. I feel like a liability."

"Did you ever think that maybe he went after you for a reason?" Atara asks. She touches Cass's shoulder and forces her to look into her eyes.

The way Cass looks at her tells me that she hadn't thought of that.

"You'll get the power that's meant for you. And, I'm sure it'll be incredible."

She turns to look at me as if she's a scientist and I'm a creature she's never seen before and was told didn't exist.

"I don't understand you."

"What do you mean?"

"You have all this power and I don't think you really want it."

I roll my eyes. "Because as strong as I supposedly am, I will always hate the price that I had to pay for it." I clench my fists. "The price we all paid. As much as I understand, it still makes me sick."

She looks at me as if she's trying to formulate a response, but she can't find the words. Atara senses the tension and gets up, pulling Cass along with her.

"Come on. Let's go find Jayce and see if he wants to come too." To Cass, she says, "We're going to try and see if there's a library or something where we can search for info about the demon."

"That actually sounds like a good idea."

"Good. After we get Jayce, we'll have to ask a guide for permission. At least this way we can contribute."

"Let's ask Gwyn. She seems like she'll agree faster than the others, especially without the two guides thing," I say.

◊◊◊

Jayce isn't in his room or at the lake when we search for him. We head to the meditation area and find a few people there, but no Jayce. It seems that since we've been banned from leaving the world, we're seeing more soul tamers. Many smile or wave, but most pay us no mind.

"This would be a good time to make friends outside of Christian and Adrian," I say.

We trek through the forest and weave through the path. I wish that I had more time to admire the vibrancy of the landscape.

"Maybe later. We're on a mission," Cass says as she seems to gain new focus.

We walk for another two minutes before we find Jayce hanging from a branch doing pull ups with hardly any effort. He's wearing a forest green tank top and shorts. On his ankles look like some weights. When I look again, I realize that he's wrapped stone around his ankles. Clever.

We watch him for about a minute before he hops down and turns to us. "What's up?" he asks casually as he begins to stretch.

"Want to come with us to learn about our history?" I ask with a smile.

Jayce gives me a soft smile back. "Nah. I'm good here. I still have some workouts to do."

"Well, can it wait? I mean we can't go anywhere anyway and we can train with you later," I say hoping to change his mind.

"I'd rather do it alone. But, thanks for the offer."

"Jayce." I pout.

"Jasmine."

We stare at each other. It doesn't seem to have any effect. I open my mouth to ask him what's going on with him, but Atara steps up.

"Why don't we just catch up with you later?"

"Yeah. That'd be best." He turns and leaps back onto the branch.

I get ready to walk away with the girls, but then I turn back and head over to Jayce. I wave Atara and Cass away for a second.

"We need to talk," I tell him with my arms crossed.

"Can it wait?" he asks, grunting from his workout. This time he does a pull up and over before hanging back down.

"No."

"Well, it's going to have to. I'm busy."

"Busy being an ass," I respond.

He drops down and stares at me. Beneath the surface, he's angry, even if his face is blank. "I'll see you later, Jasmine."

"Goodbye, Jayce," I say as I turn and walk away. I should get points for not stomping and throwing a tantrum.

"Trouble in paradise?" Cass asks when I meet back up with them.

"Shut up," I mumble.

"Maybe he's just tired of hanging with us girls. I'm sure he's lonely in his own way," Atara says softly.

"Maybe."

I know that's not it, but I'm not going to debate with them about it either.

"It's not like we sit around giggling and painting our nails," Cass responds.

"But still. It's probably not the same. I don't know. I'm just guessing," Atara answers.

I try not to let my voice betray my hurt feelings. "I guess he'll come around when he's ready."

Chapter Seventeen

*G*wyn reluctantly agreed to let us visit one of 'Libraries of the Dead.' Well, just a library, but "of the Dead" makes it sound more interesting. This one is located in the sky, a sky that's dark blue with gold clouds. It's magnificent.

The library itself is a shimmering polished black. It seems to sparkle like the stars against the blue background. It is built like a dome with high columns holding up the roof and a wide arched doorway inviting you in. But, in order to enter, one must give a piece of their aura. The library pulls it from them. Apparently, it can hurt.

We stard at the ten-foot-high entrance and wait for Gwyn to tell us what to do. She flips her hair over her shoulder and steps forward.

"Try to relax. It'll hurt less." Then, she walks through. Her body jerks as light flares around her. Then, she continues through the threshold.

Atara goes next. She grunts as she walks through and then sighs in relief. I go next. It feels like one hundred hot needles digging into my skin. Then, it disappears in less than a second. My skin still tingles as I step through. Cass goes last and with an eye roll and arms crossed acts like it didn't faze her at all.

"The library is semi-sentient. If it senses that any of the documents are being taken or destroyed, it will expel the person by searching through its energy that it's collected."

"That's scary and awesome," Atara says.

"Remind me not to accidentally rip a page," Cass mutters.

Gwyn chuckles. "I think it says a lot about you guys that you want to try to do this to help. The library is large. I'll leave you guys to the exploring. I'll be off in a corner taking a nap. Call me if you need me."

"Okay. Should we split up or..."

"Let's look around on our own for a bit, see what we find," Cass says.

I turn to actually look around. No way this place is this huge. It sure didn't look it from the outside. Magic. I decide to go all the way toward the back and work my way to the front. Maybe I can tell how old texts are based off what the paper looks like.

Before I know it, I've been sitting there reading about old stories about what the world was like when it was young and of legendary heroes. The stories contain tales of darkness and monsters that will probably give me nightmares from now on. But, I find nothing of soul tamers like August. I don't think that it's a mistake.

The Soul Kings don't want anyone to know that they either made a mistake with the demon experiments or that they have something else planned. And it makes me wonder. What if they didn't destroy them all? What if there are more out there like August fighting in the shadows, listening, learning.

I meet back up with my friends with more questions than answers.

"Any luck?" I ask Cass as she thumbs through a text.

She runs her hand through her chocolate hair in frustration. "Not at all. But, I am learning a lot."

"Well, then it's not a complete loss, right?"

"I guess not. It could be worse."

I give her a soft smile. "Are you being semi-optimistic?"

"Don't get punched," she warns.

I laugh and put my hands up in surrender.

"There you guys are," Atara says as she turns the corner. "Did you find out anything that can help us?"

"Nope and nope. You?"

"Well, I think I've got something that might be able to help."

My stomach clenches.

"What?" Cass asks before I get the chance.

"There's a list of sealed demons and their descriptions from a very long time ago. He could be on that list."

'No, he won't be because he isn't a demon,' I think. "Cool, let's see it," is what I say. I should just tell them what I know. But, I still choose to keep it a secret. I still choose to lie to my friends.

"I left it there. Come on." Atara leads us to a stack of books on the floor in a corner. We all circle up and read through the pages. Atara and Cass make several comments to each other, but I remain silent as I read through.

Many of these beings are too powerful to kill. But, if they were to get free- well, we'd have a fight on our hands. Demons of chaos, war. Spirits of destruction- enemies of peace. Of the mortal world. Any one of them could change the tide of this war.

War.

A chill courses through me.

What if Kenji's team finds August and someone gets hurt or dies? Can I prevent that from happening? What would Hector do if he were in my shoes? Why does loyalty and duty have to be opposing themes?

"Hello? Jazzy, are you listening?" Atara asks, waving a hand in front of my face.

"I'm sorry. What cid you say?"

"I asked if you've found anything?"

I hesitate and look into brown and gray eyes. "No. But all this reading is making me tired. I think that's enough for me today."

Cass nods, but Atara frowns before schooling her face into a more neutral gaze.

"Well, let's put this stuff back and go find Gwyn."

"Okay. Maybe we can do a bit of sparring on the roof," Cass suggests.

"Sure."

We clean up and set off to find Gwyn who is napping against a shelf. When we get back, I think about going to try to ask Jayce to join us again, but I decide against it. It can wait.

Our sparring consists of us working on defending ourselves against two opponents using very little power. We work on fundamentals- hand placement, using the most precise movements, reading our opponents.

But, my mind is too occupied with other thoughts and I end up taking more than a few punches.

It's obvious that Cass wants to comment on my lack of focus, but she refrains from doing so. She must be practically biting down on her tongue.

Big surprise.

They probably think it's because of Jayce.

Shortly after, we decide to all call it a night. They go to their rooms. I go to the lake. I sit on the shore with my knees to my chest as I try to clear my thoughts. There's a fog covering my mind.

About an hour passes, but it doesn't work. So, I change into a bathing suit and step into the water. I swim out far before I simply float on my back. Maybe my problems will stay on shore while I drift away.

The water begins to make me feel refreshed. But, that's only physical. My emotions are running very high. Sometimes I wish they'd just shut them off completely. I'd be a perfect robotic soldier.

Nothing's ever that simple.

I wish that I could speak to my family about this- somebody that knew me before. They'd understand my heart. They'd know that when I solve problems, I second and third guess myself all the time. They'd know that I wouldn't want to do anything to hurt anybody.

"Jasmine," I hear a whisper on the wind before he materializes on the shore. He's in his own flesh- no glamour, but even from here, his eyes shine in a red glow. It frightens me. But I still go to him.

I take a deep breath out of habit and dive under the water, pushing and kicking out with my legs to hurry to shore. I'm so nervous about his arrival that I didn't even think to just magically appear next to him.

"August?' I ask as I step onto the shore, the hint of moonlight at my back. My body drips water droplets onto the black sand.

He's holding his arm close to him and is swaying with the need to stay upright. He grimaces in pain, but tries to mask it with a smile. I'm not fooled. He should be healing.

"August, what's happening?"

"I'm losing. I'm losing."

He falls into me. He's heavier, taller. The armor adds to his weight and my knees buckle as I try to support him. His head rests on my shoulders and he tries to steady his breathing.

"I need to remember who I am. I need to remember my humanity before I destroy everything."

Hesitantly, I wrap my arm around his back. His body shakes as if he's sobbing. It must take incredible effort to maintain his composure and fight the demons inside of him while he's vulnerable.

"You can't let the demons inside you win," I whisper.

"You remind me so much of Hector. You are kind just like him. Seeing you is like meeting an old friend."

"August, you can't stay."

"Jazzy, I knew I'd find you he-," Jayce's voice calls out.

For a few seconds, the world stops. The waves stop lapping against the shore, the wind doesn't skate across my skin, and there are no sounds in the distance.

I'm in a vacuum.

Then, it speeds up again. I turn just as Jayce pulls his weapon. August pushes me away and leaps in front of me. I hit the ground just as August blocks an attack with an "x" block from Jayce's staff. His body sinks into the wet sand from the force.

Then, August pushes him away with a blow of demonic energy. He doesn't even lay a hand on him, but Jayce rolls on the ground, sand sticking to his body. The hairs on the back of my neck stand up. Everyone here probably felt that. It's too late to cover this up.

I flash in between them, my hands outstretched, my back to Jayce.

"No. Not him. Go. Now!" My power rises in warning.

His eyes shine with fear. "What will happen to you?" August asks.

"I'll be fine. Go!"

I turn to see both of them and it feels like I'm facing a firing squad.

Jayce is on his knees, staring at us in incredulousness. Then, he looks at me with eyes painted of hate and betrayal. I ignore him, but the knowledge of it still stings.

August gives me another look and then disappears.

I feel the energy of more soul tamers.

I turn to Jayce, tears in my eyes, but I don't know how they got there. "I'm sorry," I say and then I disappear. I hear him calling my name, but the wind carries it away.

I appear in the middle of my room, a sick feeling washing over me. Jayce is going to tell them that I helped him and they're going to punish me. Would they even believe me if I told them the truth? Would it matter? August clearly lacks control and sanity.

Why would he come here?

A large part of me does want to help him. A small part of me wants to trust him.

They won't understand.

I don't even understand.

Jayce comes up behind me. Surprisingly, he's alone. But, for how long?

"I thought we were friends."

I don't turn yet. I can't handle seeing him look at me that way again. "We are," I say quietly.

"Then why!" he screams at me. It feels as if the building should crumble down around us with the force of his rage.

It pains me to turn, but I finally do so after a moment. I might as well rip the Band-Aid off. I'm met with clenched fists and gritted teeth. The look is so wrong on such a beautiful face.

I give him a sad smile. "He's not the enemy, Jayce."

"He's a demon," he spits. "He nearly killed Cass and Atara. He would have. And you believe whatever lies he's been telling you just like that. You don't even know him. How did he even break through here? They said it was impossible."

"Jayce, it's complicated."

"Well, un-complicate it!"

His booming voice startles me, but then, I just get angry. I didn't ask for this.

"I can't. I just can feel it."

He chuckles. "Is this one of your special gifts? You're the chosen one, so your word is fucking gold?"

I flinch as if his words have physically cut me.

"That's what you really think of me, huh? I'm just the girl with the silver spoon stuck up my butt, arrogant, not a care in the world. That hurts, Jayce."

He points at me as if I'm the defendant in a trial and he's a witness on the stand. "You're the girl who continues to lie to her friends, Jasmine. You did that. You chose to do that. But, you're not going to do that if it means putting us in danger. I came to let you explain yourself. You won't even try to do that much. You're not even the girl that I thought you were."

I focus my energy, waiting for his answer. I coil it around me like a cobra waiting to strike. Constantly keeping my power wrapped around me has helped my focus tremendously. I know how much more powerful it's made me.

He stares me down, a clear challenge. We might as well be in a Western.

"I'm telling our-,'

A furious gale slams into Jayce before he can even finish his sentence. The bed flips over as well as my paint supplies, leaving the room in an explosion of color that drips from the walls and ceiling. He lands on the floor, out cold.

"Maybe one day, you'll understand."

I've made my choice.

I close my eyes and steel myself. Then, I disappear from this world, searching for the reason for all of this. For the person that once again has turned my world upside down.

Chapter Eighteen

Where do I go from here? Somehow, I find myself back at the beginning where Micah saved me. It feels like that was a million years ago. But now, he's the last person I need to come for me. I shut down our link and try to suppress my energy as much as I can. They've probably found Jayce by now and he's telling them everything.

What if I'm wrong about this?

He appears out of nowhere, looking like a beautiful nightmare. So wrong, yet so perfect.

"You're not wrong about me," August tells me, somehow reading my thoughts.

He looks more like himself. Sturdy, confident. He reminds me of a king the way he strides over with his sword at his side. I want to believe him. I want to believe in him.

"You can read my mind now?"

"It doesn't take a mind reader to see that you are torn, Miss Whitmore. I am very sorry that I caused you this distress. I will make it up to you, I promise. But, if you want to turn back now, I'll understand. You can tell them that I altered your mind when you went after me the first time. I'm a demon, they'll believe it." He brushes my hair back from my face.

I shiver as I realize I'm still in my swimsuit. Not cold, not really; but it's the fact that I should be. I change into a red leather jacket, white t-shirt, and black skinny jeans.

"You're not a demon, August," I tell him firmly.

"Not completely. Not yet."

"Not at all if you fight." I stare into his eyes. They're normal, brown and warm.

He changed the subject. "What are you going to do, Jasmine?"

I think back to my first vision. Then, I think about the other people out there that may be like him. Others that could really make a difference. I want to find them.

"I want to come with you. I'm going to help keep you grounded and you're going to train me and help me find others like you. They're out there. I know it. I don't know what the Soul Kings are planning, but I feel like this is where I'm supposed to be."

"Come here," he demands gently.

I step forward without question and he touches my forehead again with two fingers and runs them down to the bridge of my nose.

"Let me see you, Jasmine Whitmore."

I let him in. Memories unfold before him. Laughter during Christmas morning, playing hide and seek with Rayne, my mom and I working on art together, steering the wheel while my dad drives, learning how to swim, crying when my fish died, Rayne making fun of me when I was mad. Justin Bridges telling me he liked me, our first kiss in the hallway, Selene opening the painting I created for her, hanging out at the lake with my sister, then my fear, the murders, my death.

It's bloody and it's horrible, but I face it. I don't shy away from what happened, what brought me here. It hurts, it's terrible, but it's my story. The pages are sealed.

Suddenly, everything goes in reverse and my memories speed past again until they are no longer my own. I'm shown my mother, her life growing up, meeting my father, and more. Then, it shows my grandparents. People that moved on long before me feel like familiar friends.

I see everyone- their struggles, their growth, those that left me their legacy. They are mine. My family. I see my entire bloodline- all the way to Hector.

Then, he's standing in front of me, wide smile on his face. His hazel eyes shine with pride. He steps closer to me and reaches for my hand. Tentatively, I reach out with mine and am met with a solid, warm, calloused grip.

"H-how," I whisper.

"If you practice long enough, your powers have very few limits. We possess skills that have long been forgotten," he tells me. "When I sealed Augustus, I used some of my essence. A small part of me lingers inside of him, inside of his mind."

I want to tell him that there's already too many things inside of his mind, but instead I just nod, accepting his words.

His kind expression changes, growing serious. His eyes command my attention. "After I sealed Augustus, I begged the Soul Kings to take away everyone's memory of those that were forced to bond with the demons."

"Why?"

"Because for the most part, the experiment was a failure that need not be repeated and I couldn't bear to let my friend die because of their mistake."

"They didn't do it for free, did they?" If there's one thing my father taught me, it's that nothing is ever free.

"No. They used my power to do it. It weakened me and ultimately caused my demise. I had to use my remaining power to seal a very dangerous demon. I died and lost my flesh form. I am but another spirit now."

"I'm sorry. I don't know what else to say."

"There's nothing to say. I am unhappy that you had to suffer so. For you and Rayne as well as your parents. I wish that I could take away your pain. But, pain is strength to draw from. Soul tamers die young in exchange for tremendous power. It is both a gift and a curse. You can only be awakened through tragedy. Some can get past that, some can't. You have to decide which one you'll be."

Before I realize what I'm doing, I have my arms wrapped around him. Hector, a stranger, yet still so familiar. My family. It's a bond that stretches through time. He's the only family that I'll ever be able to touch again.

That knowledge sinks deep into my heart like an anchor plunging into the ocean. I wish to cherish this.

He returns the hug with equal warmth.

"What now?" I ask. Maybe if I keep asking, someone will decide to give me the right answer.

He pulls away. "I do not know the answer. But, Augustus knows of a place where you will not be found. You can decide what you will do until then. I have severed your connection with your soul guide. He will not find you so easily."

"Will I ever be able to talk to you again?"

"There is only a small chance. My energy inside of Augustus is nearly drained."

I frown. I want to be able to seek his advice again.

"Left unchecked, Augustus will be a danger to everyone near him. Those demons inside of him are poisoning him from within. They hope to corrupt his soul. If they gain control of his body, a host such as he will cause devastation."

"Should he even be unsealed?"

Hector's lost in thought and doesn't seem to want to answer. "It has already been done. He may be able to be contained again, or he can fight for his humanity. I will admit that sealing him may have been just as cruel as taking his life."

"Hector?"

He interrupts. "I am sorry, my child, my time runs short. We may meet again." He pulls me into another hug. "I wish I could teach you all I know. But, you'll be fine. Trust yourself. Goodbye, Jasmine, my kin."

"Goodbye, Hector." As I pull away, he disappears.

◊◊◊

I awake on a patch of grass. August is washing his upper body in a river. His hands cup some water and he splashes it over his face. The sunlight catches the droplets of water causing them to glisten in his dark hair. He looks so normal, young. Boy, can looks be deceiving.

I stand up and stretch before joining him near the water. I reach into the river and splash some on my face. The cold shocks me awake. He turns to me with a smile.

"Hey," I say.

"Hello, Jasmine."

"What happened?"

"You lost consciousness shortly after I touched your mind. I brought you here because only Hector and I know of this place. This is our sanctuary. We used a spell, created it together and cloaked it. It's almost like the world where your soul guide brought you to live. You'll be safe here. And if you decide you no longer want to stay, then you are free to leave. I will help you grow stronger, but you owe me nothing."

"I meant what happened to you, to your arm. Why did you show up like that?"

"I felt the energy of a group of soul tamers near. When I went to hide, the demonic side attempted to take over. It wanted to go hunt. I blacked out. By the time I regained control, I had a weapon piercing my arm and two others were trying to seal me."

"Did you kill them?" I ask quickly.

"I don't think so. I tried not to, but I did have to get away. I was losing my mind and I needed help. I sought you out without thinking it through. If you leave..."

"August, I'm not going anywhere. At least not yet. I betrayed my friends. I can't go back until I have something to show for it." I step back from the water and switch into my clothes that I fought with my friends in for the last time.

"Like what?"

"We need to end this war before it starts. You were right about inserting yourself among the demons. You need to do more than just infiltrate and lurk in the shadows like a bug."

He steps forward, his bottom wrapped tightly in a long cloth. Then, he shifts back into his armor, his tattoos like coal against his skin. His sword clangs at his hip. "What are you saying, Jasmine?"

I step forward and look him straight in the eye. The burden that he carries is so clear in those depths. I can almost see the demons lying in wait, clawing for control. But, I share my own burdens too, a destiny that I cannot run from.

"You're not going to slink around in the shadows, August. You're going to become a demon king and I'm going to help you. You have to become larger than life. You need a name that makes your enemies hesitate before even clashing with you.

Augustus, God Slayer, and me, the Blood Rose by your side."

"Since you seem to have an entire plan already, what do you suggest, princess?"

I smirk and call for my weapons. "We make them believe."

For the lives of my friends, the demons, the soul tamers, they will fear us.